IN THE HOUSE

"I heard you were in the hospital." She looked past me, at an emerald green vodka sign my parents had hung on the wall to give it that bar atmosphere.

"I was," I said. "But not for mono."

Her eyes flicked back to my face. I felt the question sitting on her tongue. If I tapped her on the back, it would probably pop right out. I ran my fingers over the smooth top of the bar and met her stare, daring her to ask me. And I wasn't sure why I was daring her, except that the way she'd wormed herself into my house made me curious about how far she would go. From what I'd seen, if anyone had the guts to ask me to my face, this girl would.

Her eyes fixed on mine, her lashes lifting as if she hoped I would answer without her having to say it out loud. But she broke first, glancing away.

"Come on," I said. "I'll walk you back upstairs."

OTHER BOOKS YOU MAY ENJOY

Catalyst	Laurie Halse Anderson
Dreamland	Sarah Dessen
Hold Still	Nina LaCour
If I Stay	Gayle Forman
Impossible	Nancy Werlin
Keep Holding On	Susane Colasanti
Lock and Key	Sarah Dessen
The Rules of Survival	Nancy Werlin
The Secret Year	Jennifer R. Hubbard
The Sky Is Everywhere	Jandy Nelson
Someone Like You	Sarah Dessen
When It Happens	Susane Colasanti

Try Not to Breathe

JENNIFER R. HUBBARD

speak

An Imprint of Penguin Group (USA) Inc.

SPEAK
Published by the Penguin Group
Penguin Group (USA) Inc., 345 Hudson Street, New York, New York 10014, U.S.A.
Penguin Group (Canada), 90 Eglinton Avenue East, Suite 700, Toronto, Ontario, Canada M4P 2Y3
(a division of Pearson Penguin Canada Inc.)
Penguin Books Ltd, 80 Strand, London WC2R 0RL, England
Penguin Ireland, 25 St Stephen's Green, Dublin 2, Ireland (a division of Penguin Books Ltd)
Penguin Group (Australia), 250 Camberwell Road, Camberwell, Victoria 3124, Australia
(a division of Pearson Australia Group Pty Ltd)
Penguin Books India Pvt Ltd, 11 Community Centre, Panchsheel Park, New Delhi – 110 017, India
Penguin Group (NZ), 67 Apollo Drive, Rosedale, Auckland 0632, New Zealand
(a division of Pearson New Zealand Ltd.)
Penguin Books (South Africa) (Pty) Ltd, 24 Sturdee Avenue,
Rosebank, Johannesburg 2196, South Africa

Penguin Books Ltd, Registered Offices: 80 Strand, London WC2R 0RL, England

First published in the United States of America by Viking,
a member of Penguin Group (USA) Inc, 2012
Published by Speak, an imprint of Penguin Group (USA) Inc., 2013

1 3 5 7 9 10 8 6 4 2

THE LIBRARY OF CONGRESS HAS CATALOGED THE VIKING EDITION AS FOLLOWS:
Hubbard, Jennifer R.
Try not to breathe / by Jennifer Hubbard.
p.   cm.
Summary: The summer Ryan is released from a mental hospital following his suicide attempt,
he meets Nicki, who gets him to share his darkest secrets while hiding secrets of her own.
ISBN 978-0-0670-01390-6 (hardcover)
[1. Suicide—Fiction. 2. Interpersonal relations—Fiction.] I. Title.
PZ7.H8582Try 2012
[Fic]—dc22
2011012203

Speak ISBN 978-0-14-242387-5

Set in Minion
Printed in the United States of America

This book is for those who survived,
and in memory of those who did not.

ONE

It was dangerous to stand under the waterfall, but some kids did it anyway, and I was one of them. The water pounded my mind blank, stung my skin. It hit my naked back, chest, and shoulders so hard I couldn't think. That water could knock me over, force the breath out of me, pin me to the rock, and I knew it.

But I kept doing it.

My parents' heads would've shot through the roof if they'd known. They'd done their best to wrap me in cotton since I'd gotten out of Patterson Hospital a few months before. My mother panicked if I missed a dose of my meds, so I sure wasn't going to tell her about the waterfall. How could I explain it, anyway?

Because I needed it. The roaring water shot over the ledge and beat down on my shoulders and head, a thunder I felt even through the slick stones under my feet. My nerves crackled and buzzed. It was all I could do to stand still against the water.

Whatever else I had messed up in my life, I could do that much: stand still. Okay, so I wasn't setting the bar too high.

There were rumors that a guy had drowned here once, or that he'd fallen from the cliff and smashed his head on the rocks, his brains spilling into the pool below. Each version of the story was bloodier and less believable than the last.

There were rumors about me, about what I'd done back in the spring. Everyone snuck looks at me in the school halls after I got out of Patterson. Sometimes I was tempted to foam at the mouth and babble to invisible people, because the other kids seemed so disappointed that I didn't. But I couldn't be sure they would realize it was a joke. The few times I'd tried to make anyone laugh, all I got were nervous glances and squirming. Nobody expected me to have a sense of humor, and it was safer for me to let them think I might be crazy than to give them proof.

So I knew about rumors, how they were 95 percent bullshit with maybe one kernel of truth. I wasn't sure where the kernel was in the story about the dead guy at the waterfall.

I first went under the waterfall in May, and I kept it up all summer. July was so hot, I imagined steam pouring off me whenever the icy rush hit my skin.

Early in August, we got rain. I watched the waterfall from the stream bank, waiting for the cool stormy weather to pass, for the heat to return.

I was sitting there one day when Kent Thornton's sister came by. Kent was going into eleventh grade like me, and I knew his sister was a year younger, but I'd never talked to her much. Last year she'd been at the junior high, since Seaton High didn't start until tenth grade.

"Hey, Ryan," she said, planting her feet in the moss.

"Hey." I tried to remember her name, but couldn't.

She stood watching the water charge over the cliff. Ferns waved in the breeze. "Are you going in?" she asked.

"No, not today." All that rain had swelled the creek and the waterfall. I was tempted to see if I could stand up under the cold weight of that water, but I wasn't completely insane, no matter what kids at school might whisper about me.

"I do it all the time." She grinned. "My friend Angie won't even stick her foot in the water. She says the rocks are too slippery."

"They are slippery." Not that it had ever stopped me.

Kent's sister wiped sweat off the back of her neck. "You live up at the glass house, don't you?"

"It's not glass." I hated when people called it that. It sounded like we were expecting some TV show to feature us in our architectural wonder of a home. *Lifestyles of People Who Have Way More Money Than You.* "It just has a lot of windows."

"Whatever. That's your house, right?"

"Yeah. Why?"

Her face flushed pink. "Just wondered." She waved at the waterfall. "Dare me to go under there?"

"Nah, it's too cold today. And strong. It's kind of dangerous."

She stepped into the water. Ripples spread out from her foot.

She wore a tank top and shorts, which she didn't take off. She walked toward the waterfall, slipping once on the mossy rocks.

I followed her with my eyes. Dread squeezed my stomach and wedged a lump at the back of my throat. I didn't even know this girl, but I had no desire to see her crushed, drowned. She disappeared under the silver curtain of water.

I stood up because I couldn't see her anymore. I squinted at the foaming water, trying to see into it, through it.

My fingers tapped the sides of my thighs as if counting the seconds she'd been under. How long should I wait before going in after her? If I should go in at all—there being a narrow line between heroes and idiots.

Kent's sister ducked out, spitting, hair glued flat to her head. I exhaled. She lifted a handful of wet hair off her face, shook herself like a dog, and laughed. She splashed toward me.

"You all right?" I said.

Her lips were purple; her skin prickled with goose bumps. Her teeth hammered against each other.

"I should've brought a towel," she said.

I'd done that before—remembered the towel only *after* I was wet. "I can get you one."

"Okay." She rubbed her arms. "That sounds fantastic."

I led her to my house, a ten-minute walk through the woods. I didn't know how to act: whether to make eye contact, how long to look at her, how close to walk. I didn't talk to people much, except Jake and Val, and with them I could talk about anything. What were you supposed to say to people you barely knew? That was the kind of thing I needed lessons in—forget algebra and history.

Her wet clothes dripped on the evergreen needles covering the path. A few times, she reached out to brush the white-pine needles that hung in soft bunches from the trees along the trail. "So I get to see the glass house," she said, through chattering teeth.

"Don't get your hopes up. It's not that exciting."

"It's got to be more exciting than my house."

What was she expecting—champagne fountains? A private theater? I tripped over a root, staggered a couple of steps, and decided to glue my eyes to the ground from now on.

"I think I saw you at the waterfall yesterday," she went on. "Reading. But you left while I was coming up the trail."

"Oh, yeah—I was there."

"What were you reading?"

"This book about some guys who tried to cross the Pacific Ocean on a handmade raft."

"The Pacific? On a raft?" She shook her head. "That's wild."

That was why I'd wanted to read it, but nobody else I knew seemed impressed. My dad had said, "Huh, how about that"— exactly the same response he'd used when my mother told him the price of asparagus had gone up. Val had said, "God, some people have to do everything the hard way." My friend Jake didn't seem entirely clear on which ocean was the Pacific.

"Did they make it?" Kent's sister asked. I was wishing I could remember her name now, wishing I hadn't waited too long to ask. Not only because she cared about the guys on the raft, but because she didn't choose every word as if she had to wrap it in tissue paper before she gave it to me—as if I might snap if she said the wrong thing. Which was the way practically everyone else at school talked to me.

"Not all the way," I told her. "The raft was falling apart, so they had to quit."

"That would've been amazing." After a pause: "If they'd made it, I mean."

Our house hid among the trees. It consisted mostly of vertical boards and glass. Mom said it had "clean, modern lines." She said we needed all those windows to "bring nature inside." My grandmother always told her it was hideous, too big and too stark, but nothing anyone said could dent Mom's obsession with this place. It had taken three years and an army of contractors to build. I'd spent more afternoons than I liked to remember in this yard, breathing paint and turpentine, brushing sawdust out of my hair. Mom used to chase plumbers, electricians, and carpenters around the lot while I did my homework under the trees. I developed incredible powers of concentration from studying to the background noise of hammers clanging and saws tearing through wood.

Kent's sister stood on the tiles in the front hall while I brought her two big white towels.

"Fluffy," she said. She wrung out her hair and rubbed herself with them.

"'Fresh and soft as a springtime morning,'" I drawled, quoting an asinine fabric-softener commercial that was on all the time lately, and she laughed.

■ ■ ■ ■ ■

I wanted to say more about the guys on the Pacific raft, because for days that story had filled my head, and I'd imagined I was out there on the ocean with them. But now I was thinking maybe she really hadn't cared after all; maybe she was just being polite.

"Could I look around?" she asked.

"I guess so." Mom had given tours of the house to all her friends and relatives, but I'd never paid much attention, beyond noticing how their eyes glazed over after the third room. Still, if this girl actually wanted to look through the house (to search for the nonexistent champagne fountains?), it was okay with me. "Do you want dry clothes? I could give you a T-shirt or something."

"No, thanks. I'm good."

She followed me through the living room, where one wall was made entirely of windows. The carpeting and furniture were a blank color, like vanilla, because my mother said the view should be the "focal point" of the room. Not that I mentioned focal points to Kent's sister. Not that I said anything at all, in case she was taking notes so she could tell the neighborhood what it was like inside the crazy guy's place. But all she said was "The trees are *right there*," stretching her arms toward them. "It's like living *in* the forest."

She wanted to see everything, from the bathrooms to the broom closet. Maybe the broom closet was interesting in a bizarre way, as evidence that someone in our family was a little too compulsive—the brooms and mops and sponges all lined up, the dust rags folded in a neat pile on the shelf—but otherwise I didn't see the fascination.

She marched into my room, not even pausing on the threshold.

Could she tell she was the first female under the age of forty to set foot in there? With a flip of her hand, she spun the globe on my desk. I stopped it, my fingers landing on Greenland. She studied my hand as it rested on the stopped planet, and I sensed she wasn't just inspecting the house—she was inspecting me, too. I was suddenly aware of the sound of my own breathing. Was it louder than usual, and if so, did she notice it?

I followed her eyes as they took in my computer, my bookshelves, the walls that were empty except for one painting Val had done in therapy—an abstract of blue and purple swirls. I often traced those satiny swirls as if I could touch Val's skin through them, as if she'd left part of her flesh in the painting.

"So what's the verdict?" I asked Kent's sister, tired of trying to read every blink of her eyelashes, every twitch of her mouth. I couldn't shake the feeling that she was searching for something, though I couldn't imagine what it was.

"Compared to you, my brothers are slobs. But then—compared to anyone, they're slobs."

The one thing I didn't want her to see was the package on the upper shelf in my closet. I tried to think of an excuse to keep her out of there—as if I owed her an explanation for why she couldn't see inside every drawer and cubbyhole. But she just glanced at the partly opened door. Apparently my clothes weren't as riveting as our mops and brooms, and she didn't inspect the closet after all.

She lifted a corner of the window shade and peered out. "I love your room. You are so lucky."

▪ ▪ ▪ ▪ ▪

The only door I wouldn't open was the one to my mother's office. Aside from the problem of introducing Mom to a girl whose name I couldn't remember, I didn't want to go through the whole *who is Ryan's little friend* interrogation. My mother could squeeze an entire biography out of anyone, complete with blood type and the names of first-grade teachers. So I said, "My mom's in there, working."

Kent's sister put her ear to the door. "Really?" she whispered. "I don't hear anything."

I laughed. "She's on the computer. What do you expect?" For a minute I thought she suspected me of hiding dismembered bodies in there or something. I could imagine what the kids at school would say if Kent's sister told them we had a mysterious door we never opened. But she pulled away from the door and shrugged.

We ended the tour in the basement. "Holy crap, it's like a gym down here," she said. "Do you use all this equipment?"

"I used to—especially the treadmill. Now it's mostly my mom."

Kent's sister threaded her way between the machines. She sat on the rowing machine. "Hey, we can row across the Pacific." She rowed a couple of strokes, stopped, and tilted her head up at me. "How come you don't use this stuff anymore?"

I ran my hand along the treadmill's control panel. "Last winter I got mono. I had to stop everything for a while. I used to play baseball, and run . . . and I never got back into it."

"Mono," she repeated, as if weighing that story against whatever rumors she'd heard. Her eyes were pale gray, almost light enough to see through.

"Yes," I said, not blinking. "Mono."

She stood up and headed for the far wall. Along that side of the room was a bar we never used. My parents had had a fantasy, when we moved in, that they would host regular parties down here. I wasn't sure where that idea had come from, since they'd never had parties before, and they didn't now. Kent's sister sat on a bar stool, crossed her legs, and crooked an arm, holding up an imaginary wineglass. She draped one of the towels around her neck as if it were a mink.

"Chah-ming, dah-ling," she boomed, waving her pretend glass. "Won't you pour me anoth-ah?"

I stepped behind the bar. "The booze is locked up. Not that there's much of it to begin with. But you can have all the tonic water you want."

She stuck out her tongue and gagged.

"Yeah, I know," I said. "The only thing I like about tonic is that it turns blue under black lights."

She leaned on the bar and fiddled with one end of the towel. "Did you really have mono?"

"Yes," I said.

"I heard you were in the hospital." She looked past me, at an emerald green vodka sign my parents had hung on the wall to give it that bar atmosphere.

"I was," I said. "But not for mono."

Her eyes flicked back to my face. I felt the question sitting on her tongue. If I tapped her on the back, it would probably pop right out. I ran my fingers over the smooth top of the bar and met her stare, daring her to ask me. And I wasn't sure why I was daring her, except that the way she'd wormed herself into my house made me curious about how far she would go. From what I'd seen, if anyone had the guts to ask me to my face, this girl would.

Her eyes fixed on mine, her lashes lifting as if she hoped I would answer without her having to say it out loud. But she broke first, glancing away.

"Come on," I said. "I'll walk you back upstairs."

We stood in the living room, in front of the windowed wall. Her breath misted the glass. "You have the best house."

"You should've seen it when we moved in. My parents are still suing the builder."

"Why?"

"We were only here a couple of weeks before the windows started leaking. And the roof." My mother's hovering during every minute of the construction hadn't guaranteed a perfect house after all. "We had to move out for a few weeks while it got fixed." I stopped then, because I didn't want to talk about what had happened during that move.

"Do you go to the waterfall a lot?" Kent's sister asked.

"Every day."

"A kid died there once, you know." She tapped a rapid, nervous rhythm on the window glass with her fingernail.

"You can't believe everything you hear."

"It's not just a rumor." She shook her head. "I was there.

His name was Bruce Macauley. He was, like, eight. I was six."

"You were there?"

"Yeah. Me and my brother. He slipped. Bruce, I mean. Slipped on the rocks."

"Oh." I'd pictured slipping on those rocks many times, the force of the cascade pinning my head underwater, but now I realized I'd never fully believed the rumors.

She stroked the pane, with her fingertips this time. My mother, who swooped down on every fingerprint with glass cleaner and a lecture, would've exploded.

"I still like the waterfall, though," Kent's sister said.

She gave me back the towels, the towels with her touch all over them. It occurred to me that I should've taken them before; she wouldn't have had to carry them through the house. "Bye, Ryan," she said at the door, and I wished again that I could remember her name. I twisted the towels, wanting to say more to her, but she was already gone.

TWO

I went upstairs to check my phone and computer for messages from Jake and Val, the only two people who ever sent me anything. We'd been together at Patterson Hospital, and we were all out now. For the past few months we'd kept in touch, though we lived in different parts of the state.

I had no messages from Val. I wrote her one and then erased it without sending it. I stared up at her painting on my wall, as if I could contact her that way, but my thought waves had no obvious effect on the painting—or my in-box. I went on weeding spam.

Jake had sent me a link to a video of an ostrich playing football, which was the kind of crap we always sent each other. I sent him back a clip of dancing cartoon walruses.

"You there?" he sent me. "Where you been all day?"

"Outside. Then this girl came over."

"What girl? Since when do you have a girl?"

"She's just a girl. She lives around here."

"So what'd you do to her?"

"Ha. Nothing."

"Come on, you can give me some juicy details. Even if you have to make them up."

I changed the subject. "What did you do all day?"

"What I always do. Played games until my wrists locked up. The Mom keeps nagging me to leave my room but what the hell for? If I had a fridge & a bathroom I'd never have to leave."

"I don't think you're allowed to be a recluse unless you're also a billionaire."

"I'm just $999,999,960.00 short of that goal. Maybe I should start a telethon: HELP ME BE A BILLIONAIRE RECLUSE, AMERICA."

I wondered if Jake had even left his house since getting out of Patterson in June, but whenever I asked, he made a joke of it. Val and I told him he would turn into a mole person or get rickets from lack of sunshine—well, okay, I guess we made a joke of it, too. Val and I had serious talks sometimes, but since leaving Patterson, Jake and I never did. I guess he thought it was bad enough, the stuff we could remember about each other from the hospital: the outbursts in the dayroom, the confessions in Group, the way we couldn't hide anything from anyone ever because we were around each other twenty-four hours a day. Once somebody's seen you wiping snot off your face after you've crumbled and confessed to a circle of mental patients that you hate yourself for wanting attention you can never have—well, then, you'd rather send him clips of ostriches and walruses than talk about that shit.

■ ■ ■ ■ ■

Early the next morning, I went up to the waterfall. It was cold, the air hazy with evaporating dew. Kent Thornton sat there, smoking. At first I thought it was just a cigarette, until the sweet heavy smell hit me. "Heard you saw Nicki here," he said.

Nicki, that was his sister's name. "Yeah."

"She's a nut."

My face stung. When people said things like that, I never knew if they meant it to be a dig at me or not.

"My mom says she's more trouble than me and my brother put together." He stared at the cascade, the endless fall of water. "She's a good kid, but she's all screwed up since our dad died."

I took a step back. If he was going to sit here all morning, I could hit the trails instead. I was hungry to be alone. When I was around other people, I always expected the next thing out of their mouths to cut me. Kent hadn't said five words to me at school; I wasn't that anxious for him to start talking now.

"You be careful with her, though." Kent swung his head toward me, his eyes webbed with red. "She's still my sister."

Be careful with her? All I'd done was lend her a towel. And let her inspect my house, right down to the broom closet.

Kent pointed to the thundering water. "You go under there, right?"

"Sometimes."

"Crazy shit." His voice cracked. "What the hell's wrong with you?"

Good question, Kent, I wanted to say. *How many hours do you have, to listen to the answer?*

"You couldn't pay me enough to go under there," he went on. "You could not pay me enough." He shook his head, then kept wagging it back and forth like he'd forgotten how to stop. I cleared my throat, and he stopped.

"See you," I said, and escaped down one of the trails. I came back an hour later, when Kent was gone.

That moment under the waterfall when I couldn't breathe was the best and worst. It scared me, but not in a bad way. The cold shock—the force of the water blasting me in the face—made it impossible to breathe until I moved aside. When I did, that gasp of air hit me like the first bite of food when you're hungry.

I stumbled to the bank, fell onto the moss, and closed my eyes. Water dripped off me into the moss and mud.

"I hear it's real cold under there," a voice said above me. "And kind of dangerous."

I opened my eyes. Nicki stood over me.

"I've heard that, too," I said.

She sat near my head. She smelled of sunscreen. And tangy, like oranges. I had to roll my eyes upward to see her.

"Are you just going to lie there?" she said.

"Is there something else I'm supposed to be doing?" Trying to see her from that angle gave me a headache. I let my eyes roll back to their natural place. The waterfall pounded onto the rocks in front of us, churning up foam.

"I want to ask you something," she said.

I remembered that moment in my basement when she'd mentioned the hospital. She was finally going to take my dare. "Ask away."

"Why do you come here?"

"To the waterfall?" Okay, so that wasn't the question I'd expected.

"Did you ever . . . dream about this place? Or feel like you were meant to be here? Or did anything weird ever happen to you here?"

I sat up. "What are you talking about?"

She sighed; at least, I thought so. It was hard to tell, so near the roaring water. "One time," she said, "the waterfall knocked me down so hard my head went under, and for a minute it was like I was hovering above my body, looking down at myself lying there in the water. And then the next thing you know, I was standing up. I was coughing and, you know, back inside my body."

"It probably knocked you out for a second."

"Did you ever have anything like that happen?"

"No, but—" I told her about the book I was reading. I'd finished the Pacific raft story, and now I was reading about a guy who'd been climbing one of the highest mountains in the world when he got stranded in a storm. He got so exhausted and disoriented that although he was alone, he thought someone else was with him, someone guiding him down the mountain. He even talked to the person—or whoever, whatever, it was. I'd read about cases like that before, where people alone in deadly situations had the sense of another person being with them.

"That's exactly the kind of thing I'm talking about!" Nicki said. "What do you think he saw?"

"I think he was hallucinating. He was dehydrated and probably hypothermic, too."

"And you think I was hallucinating?"

"Well, it sounds like you did smack your head."

"I would think you of all people would believe in—" She froze; her lips stopped in midcurl.

You of all people. Nicki wasn't the only one who froze; a glacial sheet covered my skin in an instant.

"What do you mean by that?" I asked as soon as my mouth thawed enough to let me. At the same moment she began, "I didn't mean—" Then we both shut up.

Nicki stared at the water, but I was watching her now. She rubbed the hem of her shorts.

"Me of all people, meaning what?" Whatever she wanted from me, I needed her to spit it out. I was tired of weighing every word she said, tired of trying to figure out why she'd started talking to me in the first place.

She spoke to the waterfall. "Did you really try to kill yourself?"

Yeah, that was the question. I'd dared her to ask it yesterday, but now I was having second thoughts. There was something in her I didn't trust, a pressure, an urgency. "Why do you want to know?"

"I—there is a reason. I'm not just being nosy." She dragged her eyes away from the water and met mine. Freckles dusted her face.

"What reason?"

"It's . . . complicated."

I stood up and veins of water ran down my legs from my wet shorts and T-shirt. She scrambled to her feet, too. "Why do you want to know?" I asked again.

Actually, it had been easy for people to figure out the truth about me. Right after I'd disappeared, the school had had a suicide-prevention assembly. And for some unknown reason my mother had gone to pick up my assignments and clean out my locker in the middle of the day, instead of after classes. And so everyone knew, even without me saying a word.

Nicki tilted her head skyward, as if the answer might be hanging from the trees or spiraling down from a cloud. "It's hard to explain." She turned her head toward the woods, leaving me to stare at the side of her face. She picked at a purple scab on her leg. I wanted to run out of there, to lock myself away from her questions and the gossip that was apparently going to follow me for the rest of my life.

But one thing held me back, a prickle of worry or conscience.

"Look," I said. "Sometimes when people ask me about this, it's because they're thinking about trying it themselves."

Nicki shook her head.

"It's fine, I mean, I'll give you my doctor's number. She's on vacation until the end of the month, but there'll be somebody in her office."

"That's not it, I swear."

"I don't mind. I've done it before. I gave her number to some kid at school I barely even know." This guy had come to me because

I was the only person at school who'd tried to kill himself—at least, I was the only one everybody knew about. Anyone else who'd tried had kept it a better secret than I could. I gave him the number for my doctor and the suicide hotline, and I also told the school counselor about him. As far as I knew, he was still alive, though I had no idea if he'd used the numbers.

Nicki did look at me then. "Some kid at school? Who?"

"I'm not going to tell you that."

"Well—I'm not planning to kill myself. That's not why I asked about you."

"Do you have a phone with you?"

She sighed. "I really don't need this, but I can see you won't shut up about it." She handed over her phone and let me enter the number. "Give me yours, too. And your e-mail."

"Why?"

"I want to send you something."

I hesitated, then typed in my information, my hand shaking. "Don't send me those joke messages that get forwarded to fifty thousand people," I said. What I was really thinking was: *Don't tell me you want to kill yourself.*

"I don't send that junk." Her voice softened. "I want to tell you something, but I can't say it when I'm with you. So I'm going to send it instead. Okay?"

"Okay."

If she was suicidal, I would forward her message right to my doctor. Not that she seemed suicidal to me, but why else would she care about my past? What could she possibly have to ask me?

The thought of Nicki stayed with me as I walked home, as I climbed up to my room to change out of my wet clothes. I had the weird sense that she was following, or rather leading, me through the house all over again. I tried to see my room the way she'd seen it: the desk clear of everything but the computer, my bed with its smooth covers, the rug with fresh vacuum lines in it. I decided she must have concluded I was an anal-retentive neat freak.

Val's painting was the only thing in my room that you wouldn't have found in a hotel room: those violent purple and blue swirls. My mother had hovered the whole time I hung it up, unhappy not only that I was driving a nail into her precious walls but also that I was polluting her decor with mental-institution art.

And there was one other thing in this room that was different, not that Nicki had seen it or would recognize it if she had. I opened the closet door, not wanting to but having to, hating the impulse that led me to get that bundle in the first place and then made me keep opening it up and looking at it, an obsessive jabbing and digging at the sorest spot I had.

I hooked an arm up and swept it off the shelf, caught it as it fell. Taking a full breath, I opened one end of the brown grocery bag.

The sweater was still in there, soft pink fabric. I couldn't tell if the faint scent of perfume was real or just a memory of how it used to smell when I first got it. I stared into the bag but didn't touch the sweater. I had the sense it would leave a poisonous film on my skin, and yet part of me wanted to touch it.

I wondered what it would be like to open this closet and find that the package had vanished, bag and all, where I would never have to look at or think about it again. I knew I should get rid of it. But I would've found it easier to yank out my own spleen.

Somehow it seemed the sweater should've changed more in the months I'd had it. The perfume was fading, but I thought the fabric should be rotting, unraveling, disintegrating. I wished it would. Every time I looked, though, it was as bright and soft as ever.

I closed up the bag and shoved it back onto the shelf.

THREE

When I got on my computer that afternoon, I was looking for messages from Val and Jake. I had one from Jake—he'd found twelve more dollars for his billionaire telethon—but nothing from Val.

I replied to Jake: "Heard from Val lately?"

He answered immediately. I didn't think he ever disconnected from his computer; he might as well have implanted it into his head. "She's busy with that student orchestra stuff."

I pictured Val back at the hospital, talking about music: leaning forward, hands flying, the words racing out of her mouth. She played piano, flute, and violin (not all at the same time). She'd even given a concert at Patterson once, in the dayroom.

Val could make music anywhere. She'd taught Jake and me to jam with her in the Patterson cafeteria, with forks and cups and trays, with our hands and feet, with combs. Some of the kitchen staff had liked our sessions. Others cut us short, scared by any initiative we showed, any unpredictability on our part. But Val got some of them into it; she talked the most sour-faced kitchen worker into shaking a pan of uncooked rice as accompaniment. She could thaw anyone if you gave her enough time.

After bullshitting awhile with Jake, I wrote a short message to Val: "Hi, what's up?"

I almost deleted it, but then I sent it. I was about to log off because I told myself I would not sit there for the rest of the day, checking my messages, waiting for her to answer, when a message came in from someone named nicki_t.

I clicked it open.

"i want to know what it's like and why you did it because my dad did it and i was hoping you could tell me why you did it and if you remember anything about what it was like. i hope that doesn't sound bad. i need to know and i don't have anyone else to ask."

Her dad? Shit.

For a minute I sat paralyzed, stomach curdling, reading Nicki's words over and over.

"i want to know what it's like and why you did it . . ."

She wanted to hear about the worst day of my life.

I had talked about that day exactly twice: to the people in the emergency room right after it happened and to my Group at Patterson. When I was in the emergency room, I didn't care what I said or whom I told. The second time was different; I'd grown a shell around that day and didn't want to look inside it. But they cracked me open one day in Group, and I'd poured myself out onto the Patterson Hospital floor like a puddle of raw egg.

It had taken Val and Jake hours to scrape me off that floor. I remembered them hovering, Jake's hand on one of my shoulders and

Val's on the other. Their voices rambling, soothing, Val stopping once in a while to snap at anyone else who came too close. They both missed dinner that night because I couldn't move and I asked them not to leave me.

"Of course not, we're not going anywhere," Val had said.

"We're not hungry," Jake added, though his stomach kept gurgling and groaning.

"This floor is cold," I said.

"Do you want to get up? The aides will help us if you want."

"I don't want anyone else to come near me."

"Okay," Val said.

"Just you guys."

"Okay."

"Though if you were smart, you'd both run the hell away from me."

"I hate to break it to you, Ryan, but you're not even the sickest person in this hallway."

"I am so fucked up. Can you believe how fucked up I am?"

"It's okay, Ryan."

"There's stuff you don't even know."

Val squeezed my shoulder.

"I can't do anything right. Including killing myself. Don't leave, okay?"

"We won't."

And so it went, for hours, me saying every stupid and pathetic thought that popped into my head, and saying them over and over. I don't know why Val and Jake didn't smack me to shut me up. I had no filter, no pride, no dignity. I was a raw nerve, a sniveling bundle of need.

That was the last time I'd talked about it.

I wished all Nicki had wanted was my doctor's phone number. It would be so much easier to pass her off to the professionals. It would be so much easier if she weren't asking for this chunk out of me—especially since I had no idea what she would do with it. I was sorry about her father, but did she really believe anything I told her could help?

I sent her the easy reply: "I don't like to talk about it."

She sent back: "please." That word almost got me, those lower-case letters like she was whispering or pleading.

My mother had me bring her dinner upstairs, where she ate in front of her computer. She only had to report to her regular office once a week. Most of the time, she was home. Her job title was something like Branch Supervisor for Contracts Oversight. Whatever it meant, it required her to be plugged into her computer forty hours a week, sometimes more.

"I'm sorry I can't eat with you, but this project is on a tight deadline. I told them last week we were running behind, but—" She sighed. "Louisa Rossi refuses to stick to the schedule. Why don't you eat up here, with me?"

"I already ate."

"You did? Including your vegetables?"

"Yeah."

She cut each baby carrot into quarters and chewed one bite at a time. I stood in the doorway, up on my toes and ready to bolt, while she ran through her checklist. I supposed I was lucky she didn't outfit me with a camera or a tracking chip.

"Did you take your medication this morning?"

"Yes. You saw me."

Mom swiveled her chair toward me and dug her toes into the gray carpet. She wore a skirt, as if she were at a real office, but never shoes.

She inspected my face, looking for telltale signs—of trouble, I supposed. It was part of our daily routine. She smiled, a smile crooked with hope and worry. Since my days at Patterson, my mother always seemed to be on the verge of tears when she smiled at me, so every time she did it was like another bar of iron sitting on my chest. I looked away and tried to breathe.

"All right," she said, releasing me.

I didn't hear from Val until the next morning. The sight of her name on the screen sent an electric surge through me. As usual, she didn't bother with hi-how-are-you but jumped right in: "I cut my hair."

Okay, maybe I would've preferred a message about how she couldn't live without me, but it was a message and it was from her.

"What's it look like now?" I asked. The first thing I'd ever noticed about Val was her hair. When I met her, she had hair down to her shoulders on one side of her head, and down to her chin on the other. I figured it was a crazy person's haircut, until I realized Val was one of the sanest people at Patterson. She'd cut her hair like that for fun, she said: to be unique, to be different. Who said hair had to be symmetrical, anyway?

She sent me pictures: front and back. From the front I thought she'd cut it all to chin length, but in the back, a big triangular piece had been cut out. It looked like a very pointy-nosed shark had taken a bite out of her hair. I saved the pictures to look at again later.

"My dad says it looks like my hair went through a giant ticket-puncher," she wrote.

"That's what's nice about it."

She sent me a laughing face.

"What else is going on?" I asked.

"Like what?"

"Your family. Guys." Sweat welled out of my skin when I wrote "guys." I couldn't help thinking of Amy Trillis whenever I talked to a girl. Not that Val would deliberately knock me down the way Amy had—at least I didn't think so—but if Val liked someone else, it would be a knockdown whether she meant it that way or not.

But Val answered, "Family's same as always. Mom nagging. No time for guys."

I exhaled.

"You?" she wrote.

"No time for guys here either."

"Ha. Girlz? Cmon, gimme details. I will live vicariously thru your adventures!"

My adventures—that was a laugh. "Nothing to tell." But then I thought of Nicki—not as a girl girl, in the way Val meant, but because I couldn't forget her last message.

"There's this girl," I wrote.

"Yesssssss . . . do tell . . ."

"I found out her father killed himself, & she wants to talk to me about it."

"Does she know about you?"

"The whole school knows about me."

Before Val could reply, I wrote: "She asked why I did it."

Since I'd left Patterson, nobody besides Dr. Briggs had ever asked me the questions Nicki had. At least, they'd never asked straight out. Sometimes people hinted, as if to say they wouldn't mind hearing gory details if I felt like puking out a few. But nobody had asked about that day in the garage.

Now I wrote, about Nicki, "What does she want from me, anyway?"

And Val answered, "Maybe she just needs a friend."

Val Ishihara knew about people needing friends. She was the first person I'd spoken to back at Patterson, other than the counselors. I'd been there maybe a week, and she talked to me every day. She always left an opening for me to answer, but if I didn't, she went right on carrying her side of the conversation.

"What are you doing here?" I asked her, when I finally began to speak. We were sitting in Patterson's dayroom, where she leafed through stacks of stained sheet music, trying to organize the pages. "You seem too normal for this place." Val had little tics: she picked at her nails and scalp, played with her hair, jiggled her foot. She ducked her head and talked to the floor when she got nervous. But she wasn't like the kids who thought the government had planted spy devices in their brains. She didn't curl up in a ball under her bed, the way I had done my first day.

She laughed. "You should've seen me when I first got here. I was a walking anxiety attack. I could barely even make up my mind to go to the bathroom."

In Group she always talked about panic attacks, obsessive worry, getting stuck in repetitive movements. She'd pulled out her eyebrows and half her eyelashes one year in junior high. She'd bitten the skin around her fingernails, peeled it back to show the raw red underlayer, gnawed until she bled. If she wanted to cross the room but couldn't decide whether to step first with her left foot or her right, she would stand frozen for hours. She came to Patterson when her anxious obsessions kept her from showering, eating, and even using the bathroom. That's what she said. Watching her, I wasn't sure I believed it.

"Why?" I said. "I mean, why did you get that way in the first place?"

She shrugged. "I'm only starting to figure it out. It's never going to be like a math equation: a plus b equals anxiety attack; c minus d equals I'm cured."

"I know," I said. "My mother's been looking for the magic formula ever since I came here. She thinks she can find the Moment Where It All Went Wrong."

"And what are you looking for?"

I could've said I didn't know, or that I was looking for a way to die, or that I was looking to feel okay again—all of which were true, and all of which I'd told the counselors there. But I wanted to tell Val something different—just as true, but different. Keeping my eyes on her hands, on her bitten nails and calloused fingers, I said, "I used to want to fly."

"What, like a pilot? Fly a plane?"

"No, not a plane." You had to stay behind glass and metal when you flew a plane. "I mean, really fly."

The minute I said it, I felt like an idiot. She would think I wanted to be a bird or a superhero, both of which sounded exactly like I belonged here in a mental hospital. But she stopped shuffling pages and said, "That would be so cool." She closed her eyes for a second, as if to feel the wind in her face.

For months I'd lived behind what felt like a pane of glass, separated from the world, but the transparent shield began to crack then. Maybe it was my new meds kicking in, or maybe it was the way Val listened without judging whether what I said was what she expected me to say. But we stuck together after that. And when Jake arrived a few days later, looking as panic-frozen as I'd been when I first got there, we took him in, too.

Only once did I see Val act like she belonged at Patterson. One day on our hall, she erupted. I never found out why. I was in the dayroom with Jake when we heard a crashing and banging in the hall. Jake hid under a chair—he was still at the point where he couldn't handle any turbulence—but I stuck my head out the door and saw kids fleeing from Val. A plastic tray from the cafeteria lay on the floor, and I guessed she'd thrown it. The aides crept up to her, talking in low soothing voices, the way you'd talk to a wild animal. I knew they would drag her to the Quiet Room when they caught her.

But she burst into tears and collapsed onto one of the orange-flowered couches in the hall. When the aides approached her, she held up a hand to ward them off. The rule was that if you weren't being violent, if you weren't damaging anything or anyone, you didn't have to let people touch you. Some kids stared and some giggled and some ran. Some folded into their own world. I edged up to Val's couch, expecting her to hold me off with that upraised hand, but she let me sit on the cushion, next to her head.

I held my palm over her hair, but not touching. She didn't flinch. I lowered my palm by millimeters, watching her. She sobbed as if her insides were shredding. I touched her shiny black hair, and she let me.

She cried so hard it made my own throat hurt, a sound like metal scraping asphalt. It shook me to see Val like this, because she'd always seemed so together.

All I did was pat her head. I didn't know what else to do. I was ready to sit on that couch with her for a hundred years if I had to. And she cried until nothing else would come out.

Later I asked why she had let me near her. "Because you were the only one who didn't just want me to shut up," she said.

"We used to talk every day," I typed now, to Val. "I think I miss you." In fact I knew I missed her, but it was hard enough to say it the way I had.

"I miss you too, but you live there and I live here, so . . ."

Yeah, there was the problem: the miles stretching out between us. "How's your music going?" I typed, which set her off for a long time. I sat back and watched her words scroll by, loving every one of them, wanting to pluck them off the screen and put them in my mouth.

▪ ▪ ▪ ▪ ▪

After I got off the computer with Val, I threw myself on my bed, thinking of that day I'd stroked her hair while she cried. And later, the time we'd stood together in the hall and she'd circled my wrist with her hand. I put my hand on my wrist, trying to feel what she'd felt, to call up the weight of her touch. A hot thread traveled from that spot up my arm, into my chest, down to my stomach, downward, spreading warmth the whole way.

I sat up. I would've opened my window, but the A/C was on. I sat for a few minutes, backing away from the inner heat I'd raised. When my skin had cooled, I went downstairs.

I hiked out to the waterfall and stayed in it until the chill of the water made me shake. I came out positive I was turning purple. At least I'd brought a towel this time.

Nicki showed up while I was rubbing my skin, trying to warm it.

"Oh, hey," I said. I stopped drying myself, startled at the sight of her, fumbling for the right thing to say.

"I wanted to tell you—" she began, but my words stumbled over hers.

"I'm sorry about your dad," I said.

Her mouth puckered; her face went pink. "I'm sorry about the message I sent you. I'm sorry if it was pushy."

"No, it's . . ." I watched her balance on one leg, like a flamingo; she kept her eyes on the dirt. "It's okay," I said.

"I shouldn't have bothered you."

"It wasn't—"

"It's just that I never had anyone to ask before. I was seven when my dad died, and everyone thought I was too young to talk about it. But then, later on, they all wanted to leave it alone and not drag up the past. So I read a couple of books and stuff, but they never told me what I wanted to know." She raised her eyes, frost gray, to meet mine. "Anyway, I've figured out another way to find out about him."

I tugged on my wet shirt. "What's that?"

"I made an appointment down in Seaton."

"An appointment for what?"

She stepped closer, close enough for me to catch the scent of oranges. She lowered her voice, as if the squirrels might be taking notes on us. "I found a psychic who talks to the dead. I'm going to see her tomorrow."

"You're kidding."

Nicki shook her head.

"But you know that stuff's all crap, right?"

"No, it isn't."

"Come on." I almost snapped my towel at her. "Don't go. It's a waste."

"She's supposed to be really good. My friend Angie went to see her last spring. Angie's grandfather spoke through the psychic and talked about this dog they used to have that played Frisbee. There was no way the psychic could have known that."

Anybody could guess that a person had a dog. It wasn't like the psychic had seen a three-headed unicorn. "Bull," I said.

"How can you say that? There has to be *something* to it."

"Why—just because people want there to be?"

She frowned and pinched her lower lip. It was then I noticed she'd painted her nails royal purple. "So you only believe in what you can see, what's right here, and that's it?"

"I believe in plenty of things I haven't seen. I believe I have a liver and I've never seen that."

She waved a hand, her nails a grape-colored blur. "I don't mean that. Haven't you ever had a dream that came true, or thought of someone the second before they called you, or—"

"That's coincidence."

She frowned, and I could almost see her brain searching, straining for another argument. "You already admitted there are things we can't explain, right?"

"Right, but you have to think about what makes the most sense. The simplest thing, the most likely explanation." I twisted my towel. I was about to mention Occam's razor when she cut me off.

"But you don't know for sure."

"I know that if dead people could speak, they'd talk about something a lot more important than dogs playing Frisbee."

"Says who? Maybe they can't describe the afterlife in words we can understand. Maybe they're caught between worlds when they talk to people who are still alive."

A week ago, I hadn't even known this girl's name, and now we were trading views on the afterlife. I couldn't believe I was having a conversation that involved the words "caught between worlds."

"This 'psychic' is just going to feed you general bullshit that could apply to anyone. And then she'll take your money—how much is she charging you, anyway?"

"None of your damn business."

"Fine," I said, "but I'd be real careful how much I paid her if I were you."

She put her hands on her hips. "You want to give me advice, but you don't want to help me when it counts."

I swallowed and turned my head. I told myself she wasn't my problem. But I heard the message she'd sent me, those small letters like a whisper in my brain, that "please." I told myself I didn't owe her anything. And yet, anytime someone told me they knew a person who'd killed himself, my stomach went heavy with guilt, as if I were personally responsible for all the suicides of the world. *Why do you people put us through this?* was the question I heard, whether they meant it that way or not.

"I'm trying to help you," I said, "but you don't want to listen."

"Look, if there's even a chance this person could give me some answers, I'm going to try it. That's all I'm doing, is trying."

"Yeah, but be careful. If you *want* to believe, they'll use that against you, get you to think—"

"How do you know so much about it?"

"I read this book a couple of years ago about a guy who exposed a bunch of fake psychics—"

"You read a lot, don't you." It wasn't a question. "Come out and join the rest of us in the real world for a change."

"You're the one who's not living in the real world."

She tried to stare me down then, the way she'd tried the other day in my basement. But I was much better than she was at freezing, keeping my eyes steady. Nicki's mouth quivered and I knew she would blink first, and yet—

And yet, I didn't think I could talk her out of this. She was going no matter what I said. She had plunged into the waterfall and then into my house, and now she was going to plunge right through the wall between life and death, if she had her way. But I didn't believe she would—that anyone could—punch through that barrier.

"Is somebody going with you, at least?" I asked. "Angie?"

"Angie's at her grandmother's all summer. I'll be fine."

"You shouldn't go alone. You don't even know this woman."

Her eyebrows arched. "Well, who's going to come with me? You?"

I wound the towel around my hand. "No, I—"

"Then shut up about it." She turned and took one step away from me before I reached out and touched her arm with the towel.

"Maybe I could come," I said.

"Why, so you can play watchdog?"

"If you want to call it that. Yeah," I said, dry mouthed. "I'll play watchdog."

"Okay then. Tomorrow at one o'clock."

FOUR

That night, I stood on the deck, searching for bats and fireflies. I hung over the deck railing to study the shadows under the porch, the blood pooling in my head.

My mother's voice cut into my daydreaming. "What are you doing, Ryan?"

I lifted my head: a woozy rush. "Nothing." My standard answer, designed to hold up my end of the unspoken conspiracy Dad and I had to keep her from getting an ulcer.

She stood in the doorway, her face pinched. "I asked what you're doing."

"Not trying to jump, if that's what you're worried about." We were only one story up. Even I wasn't stupid enough to try to kill myself from this height. At worst I'd jam an ankle.

She flinched.

"Sorry," I said.

If I'd said that in front of Dr. Briggs, she would have made my mother and me dissect it, pull apart everything we'd said to hunt down each hidden (and not-so-hidden) meaning. Why had I said it? What did my mother think about it? Why had she flinched? What did I think about her flinching? And in the days right after I'd gotten out of Patterson, Mom never would've let a statement like that pass. But now she changed the subject.

"Your father will be home tomorrow—if those thunderstorms in New York don't hold him up. Although I'd rather have them ground the planes than fly in that kind of weather. I don't know if they'll even let him take off from London if it's such a mess here . . ."

After a full analysis of the weather and air traffic on both sides of the Atlantic, she trailed off. "Don't you want to come inside?" she asked.

"Not yet."

She hesitated another minute before sliding the glass door shut. But she stood in the living room, waiting. I waited, too; she didn't move. I hated being watched that way.

Heat gathered in my leg muscles, compressed energy. I shook my legs out and realized they wanted to run. For weeks I'd thought about starting to run again, and I'd been on the verge of doing it, but something kept stopping me. But tonight all I felt around me was the summer air.

When the mosquitoes needled my skin faster than I could slap them, I came inside. "Well," Mom said brightly, "going to bed now?"

"I guess."

She watched me climb the stairs. "Show's over," I mumbled, but not loud enough for her to hear.

Upstairs in my room, I checked for messages. I would've loved to tell Val about Nicki's plan and see if she thought the whole idea was as crazy as I did, but she wasn't around.

Nicki had told me to come to her house. Kent would drive us into Seaton and drop us off. Not that Kent knew we were on a secret psychic mission to contact his dead father. He had something else to do in town, and Nicki had threatened to disembowel me if I told him what our appointment was for.

The Thorntons lived down on Route 7, in a box of a house with a lawn that was more dirt than grass. Someone had once brought a pile of mulch or compost to the yard, as if planning a project, but the lump had sat there long enough to sprout weeds.

Kent's eyebrows rose when he saw me with Nicki, but he didn't say anything. He jingled his keys and nodded at the car, inviting us to get in. Nicki got in front and fiddled with the radio. I sat in back. She turned up the music so loud that Kent couldn't have talked to us if he wanted to. The road shimmered, seemed to melt.

I tried to read tension or worry or hope or anything at all in the back of Nicki's head, but I was clueless. I tried to picture the psychic, and I was clueless there, too. I imagined a woman in bright robes leaning over a crystal ball, but—did they really do that? Or was that just on TV?

Seaton was the kind of place people meant when they said America was becoming one long series of chain stores. It had gas stations, fast-food restaurants, dry cleaners, big-box stores, and nothing you couldn't find in a thousand other places. If you blacked out and woke up in Seaton, you'd have no idea where you were, or what part of the country you were in.

Kent dropped us outside the post office. The August air rolled up off the road in blurry waves, scorching my lungs. I wished we were on my deck, listening to the cicadas drone. Or at the waterfall, with cold foam spilling over us.

Nicki twined her fingers together and said, "Let's go." Her voice shook, and I thought about taking her hand to calm her down. But I didn't see how I'd get my hand in between hers, to break up that nervous clench. I never touched people, anyway.

We walked behind the post office and some warehouses. Empty plastic bags and food wrappers blew past our feet. The sidewalks were crumbling, weeds thrusting up through the cracks. The sun weighed on our shoulders; my shirt was wet already. Clear drops gathered on Nicki's skin.

I was curious about how this psychic would work, what she would say, whether I would catch her in any obvious tricks. "The main rule," I said, "is that you don't tell her anything. Let her tell you."

"I know! Give her a chance."

We came to a row of short fat brick houses penned behind chain-link fences, and Nicki began counting addresses. I wanted to ask her if the psychic was so gifted, why didn't she predict the winning lottery number and move into a better neighborhood, but I bit my tongue. Anyway, I figured psychics must get that lottery question all the time; they probably had some canned answer for it.

"This is it," Nicki said, as a cheese-cracker wrapper brushed against her ankle. We walked up to the door of a brick house. She pressed the bell.

"You okay?" I asked her.

"Yes," she snapped.

I'd been wrong about the robes and crystals. We didn't get incense, a dark room, or eerie music in the background. Instead, a round little woman with glasses let us in. She reminded me of Jake's grandmother, who used to visit him at Patterson. We stepped into a living room with twenty zillion china figurines lined up on shelves all over the walls. Snowmen, ballerinas, dogs, cats, horses, unicorns, flowers . . . My eyeballs rolled, trying to take them all in.

Nicki and I stood staring at the figurines (which stared back at us) while the psychic waited in front of two egg-colored couches that were totally overshadowed by the shelves. She didn't try to speak to us yet. Apparently she'd learned that her guests needed figurine-acclimation time.

"Wow," Nicki said at last.

"Do you like them?"

"Um—sure. They're cute."

"You're Nicki," the psychic said. Then she raised her eyebrows at me.

I wanted to make her guess who I was, to test her powers, but Nicki said, "This is my friend Ryan."

"Welcome. Please, have a seat."

We sank into the giant, stale-smelling sofa cushions.

"Thanks for meeting with me, Mrs. Hale. Or do you—what

should I call you?" Nicki's voice had gone up an octave, as if she'd grown younger since we'd walked in the door. Her hands squeezed each other.

"Please, call me Andrea," the psychic said.

Andrea Hale. So she wasn't called anything like Madame Zorelda. And she kept smiling that grandmotherly smile, as if she were about to offer us fresh-baked cookies instead of an audience with the dead.

Nicki dug in the pocket of her shorts and peeled off sweaty bills. Money up front, of course.

Andrea tucked the money into a drawer and sat on the other couch. "With whom do you wish to speak?"

I spoke up then. "Shouldn't you tell us that?"

Andrea smiled. "There are many souls who might wish to speak with you. It will save time if I can focus on someone specific."

Even though I didn't believe any of this for a minute, my skin prickled when she said that about souls wishing to speak with us. I couldn't help picturing hordes of dead people massing at the gates. Maybe they would take over the figurines, and we'd have a storm of little china animals flying through the room.

"My dad," Nicki said. "His—his name was Philip Thornton."

Andrea nodded and closed her eyes.

An old window air conditioner grumbled and clacked in the background. Nicki shivered beside me but it wasn't from the A/C, because it must've been close to eighty in that stuffy room. I glanced up at the shelves, at all the black-dot staring eyes on the china figurines, and glanced away again.

Andrea's forehead wrinkled. Her lips worked. Nicki kept holding her breath, running out of air, and then gasping. I let my knee inch toward hers, not touching her, but close enough to remind her I was there.

Andrea's eyes stayed closed. A truck rumbled down the street, shaking the house. The china figurines rattled, watching us. I thought again about them coming to life. Maybe they stampeded through the house at night. Then I realized that if I kept thinking that way, I'd end up back at Patterson.

"Philip is here," Andrea said.

My eyes darted around the room, looking for a shadow, a mist, a stirring in the air. Nothing.

Nicki exhaled. She blinked, tears gathering on her lashes, and I willed her not to believe so soon, not to jump into the pool without checking for water. She said, "Um—yes, does he—remember me?"

Silence. Then Andrea smiled. "Yes, of course. You're his daughter; he would never forget you." She chuckled. "He's laughing a little that you think he would forget—but underneath it he's sad. Sad that you didn't have more time together."

Nicki dug her nails into her palms, leaving purple marks. "Ask him why he did it."

A pause. "'Why he did it,'" Andrea repeated.

Yeah, I thought. *Not many clues in that, are there, Andrea? Now what are you going to make up?*

"Yes," Nicki said, her voice firm.

Andrea's voice faltered. "He doesn't think—he can explain it.

He wishes . . . It's complicated, and he's not sure you would understand . . ."

"I *don't* understand. That's why I'm here." Nicki drew one
hand across her cheek, where the tears had spilled over.

"He wants you to know he loves you."

"Yeah, I know that! I know that. I need to know why he—" I
stepped on Nicki's toe before she could give away any more clues.
She glared at me. Her face had gone blotchy, her eyes pink. "I need
to know why he did what he did."

Andrea kept wrinkling her forehead, as if she could squeeze an
answer from the air by pure concentration. "He's sorry," she said.

"That doesn't tell me anything!" Nicki's voice broke on the
last word; the jagged edge of it seemed to cut me. I'd been wanting
her to see how useless this was, to see that Andrea was a fake. But
now I was willing Andrea to find Nicki's father, or at least to come
up with something convincing. I focused on Andrea's face, trying
to beam thought waves at her.

"He—his voice isn't clear now. Let me see if I can get him
coming in stronger."

Yeah, you'd better, I thought. *Come on, Andrea.*

The air conditioner clanked and groaned. Nicki sniffled. My
legs twitched; I wanted to jump off this couch and run.

"Daddy," Nicki said.

That's when I opened my mouth.

"Ask him if maybe he didn't mean to go so far," I said.

Andrea hesitated.

"Ask him if he—didn't see any other way out at the time."

After a beat, Andrea nodded. "It's something like that, he says."

Nicki sucked in her breath.

"Like, maybe he didn't think he could tell anyone else what was going on," I added. How much longer would it take for Andrea to pick up her cue? Weren't psychics supposed to be good at reading people?

"He was wrapped up in the pain of the moment," Andrea said, finally catching the huge softball I'd thrown her. "He didn't see the future, the consequences."

I couldn't seem to shut up, now that I'd started. "Ask him, did he just not know what else to do."

"He would go back and do it differently if he could."

Nicki watched us, her head swinging back and forth. "Oh my God," she said.

I'd overplayed, and I knew it. I'd talked too much, made the cue too obvious. But I knew there was something true in what I had said. Hey, maybe her father was speaking through me instead of Andrea. Wasn't that what Nicki had wanted? Wasn't that what she'd asked me for?

Nicki waited until we were out on the sidewalk again to pound my arm with her fist. "Are you happy now?"

"What?"

"Don't act dumb."

"Nicki—"

"So you were right, she was a fake. Does that make you feel better?" She kicked an empty beer can into the brick wall of a house.

"What makes you say she was a fake?"

"Oh, come on! It was so obvious. You fed her everything."

"I don't know what you're talking about." But I heard the lie in my own voice.

"Were you making fun of me?"

"No."

She sobbed. I sat her down on a low crumbling wall in front of a warehouse.

"She was so bad I couldn't even pretend to believe her."

"I'm sorry," I said.

"I bet."

"No, I mean—I thought it would turn out like this, but I didn't *want* it to. I wish you'd gotten what you wanted."

I let her wipe her face on my T-shirt sleeve. She turned runny pink eyes on me. "Why did you feed her that stuff, anyway?"

"I don't know."

"Did you think you were fooling me? I'm not stupid!"

"I didn't think it through. It just—came out."

"Now I'll never know why he did it."

"He probably couldn't tell you that even if he was right here."

She sniffled. "He could've left a note or something. Why didn't he? God!"

She rubbed my damp sleeve. I was thinking about *why*, and how complicated that question was, when she spoke again.

"Did you write a note?"

"What?"

"Did *you* write a *note*?"

The steamy weather wrung sweat out of me, but somehow my mouth was dry. "No."

"Why not? Why the hell not?" She got up and paced in a tight circle, kicked the wall I was sitting on.

"Look, this isn't about me."

"You made it about you, didn't you? You sure as hell made it about you in there." She pointed back at the psychic's house.

"I wanted you to get something out of going there. Andrea was flopping like a dying fish. I told you, I didn't think it through."

"Yeah, you sure didn't." She wiped her face with the bottom of her T-shirt, giving me a flash of dark-blue bra. She didn't seem to notice or care. "So you gave my father—excuse me, the imaginary ghost of my father—all *your* reasons."

"Who says they were my reasons?"

She snorted. "What else would they be? You didn't pull all that stuff out of nowhere."

Everything drained out of me then; I could hardly hold my head up. I bent over and rested my elbows on my knees. She frowned, turned away, and kicked a chunk of brick down the sidewalk. I didn't let myself think about whether she was right, whether the words I'd put in Andrea's mouth had been my own. After all, Nicki's father couldn't possibly have made the same mistakes I'd made, couldn't have lugged around the same shame I carried. Maybe he'd felt what I'd felt—that bleak pit of numbness—but he hadn't had an Amy Trillis or a Serena. He'd never hidden a pink sweater in his closet. He hadn't done the things I'd done; I would bet on that.

FIVE

We had another half hour before Kent picked us up. Nicki bought a grape juice and I bought a Coke and we sat on a bench outside the post office, watching people run in and out. The corners of Nicki's mouth turned purple from the juice, but the pink in her face and eyes was fading. She would look normal by the time Kent met us.

I wanted to ask about her father, to know more about the person whose spirit we had tried to raise, but I didn't want to set her off again now that she'd stopped crying. I couldn't picture my own father not being around. Even though he traveled all the time, at least I knew he was somewhere on the planet, walking around and talking and thinking. Somewhere he was in a business meeting, pushing his glasses up his nose and smoothing his tie, or else he was sitting in a foreign restaurant clearing his throat and blinking the way he did when he had to eat food he didn't like. Or maybe he was in an airport, checking baseball scores from his computer—he was supposedly coming home today. But if I wanted to hear his voice, all I needed was a phone. I didn't need psychics to call him up.

I looked sideways at Nicki. She tilted her bottle, and the last purple inch of juice rippled back and forth.

"I can't believe school starts in a couple of weeks," she said. "You're gonna be a junior, right?"

"Yeah." If she wanted to back away from talking about dead fathers, that was okay with me. Val and Jake and I used to do that at Patterson, let one another talk about nothing when something was too much. You could hear it in people's voices, when they got close to breaking: a tight strangled sound in the throat, their words coming out thin and wooden. Maybe that tightness was what made Nicki gulp down all that juice.

"Did you miss a lot of school when you—you know—went in the hospital?" she asked.

"Yeah, but I made it up. I came back in May, and I did extra work until July so I wouldn't get held back."

"I'll be at the high school, too, this year. Who do you hang out with there?"

"Nobody special."

She slurped from the bottom of her bottle. "Don't you have any friends?"

I knew people, but I wouldn't say I had friends at this school. I wasn't sure what stopped me. It was true I was known as the kid who'd tried to kill himself and spent several weeks in the loony bin, which didn't make me Mr. Popular—but more than that, it was just easier not to risk anything with anyone else. I didn't need friends at school anyway, since I had Jake and Val. I told Nicki, "Yeah, a couple of kids I met in the hospital."

"Are they, like, crazy?"

"Right. We get together to drool and whack ourselves on the head. It's real crazy-people bonding."

A mail truck lumbered past us, spewing fumes. We held our breath, and when the truck had turned the corner, Nicki said, "I didn't mean it that way. Are they still in the hospital?"

"No, we're all out. Val got out first—" I stopped, remembering the time Val had come back to Patterson. The recital she'd given in the dayroom. Her hand on my wrist.

"What?" Nicki said, seeing that I wasn't fully with her anymore.

I shook my head. "Just thinking of something." And Kent pulled up then, stopping the conversation.

Nicki played with the radio until Kent barked at her. I leaned my forehead on the car window, still back in that April night at Patterson when Val had come to visit. Seeing her come into the hospital as an outsider, one of Them and not Us, I could barely even speak to her. A ball of acid sat at the top of my throat the whole time she was there. I didn't want to go to her recital, but Jake had herded me into the dayroom with the others.

"How come we're using the dayroom at night?" I snapped, but he didn't hear. He went and sat right up front, while Val warmed up at the out-of-tune piano, grimacing as she always did at the fuzzier notes.

I sat in the back, near the window. I didn't turn on the lamp next to me, but there were enough other lights on so that all I could see out the window was a reflection of myself, and the dayroom with the other psychos. And even though Val's music pulled at me like a rip current, even though some of the people around me cried, and my eyes stung and my throat hurt, all I could think was how much I hated her, and I would not look at her and I would not listen to her music. I thought that even as the music filled me.

I had missed her. I'd never stopped looking for her in those halls. There was always a big empty spot next to me in the dining room, in Group, in the dayroom, in the yard. Yet I stayed in my seat when the recital was over, my legs heavy, until I could trust myself to pass her with a blank face. People crowded around her, including Jake. She was talking to them when I slipped out of the dayroom. But she followed me into the hall and tapped my arm.

"Hey, weren't you going to say hello to me?"

"Hello."

"What's wrong?"

"What makes you think something's wrong?"

"Well, the whole time I played you sat there with your arms crossed, staring out the window. Looking incredibly pissed off." Her voice softened. "What is it? Talk to me."

"You don't get it," I said, refusing to meet her eyes.

"Don't get what?"

I focused on the Exit sign across the hall. "It was nice of you to come play for us pathetic shut-ins, but you can go back out to your regular life now."

That's when she grabbed my arm, circled my wrist, and my pulse beat against her hand. She said, "I'm still—"

Her touch had glued my tongue to the roof of my mouth, but I wrenched it free and croaked, "Still what?"

"I'm still your friend. God, Ryan, it's only been a week! Do you think I'm going to forget you and what it's like in here? Do you think I *want* to forget?"

"Why would you want to remember?"

"Because it's part of me. Because I love you and Jake."

I shook my head. It didn't matter if it was a week or an hour: she'd crossed that line. She was out there now, in the regular world, and I was stuck here, still sick.

"Why do you think I came back here today?"

"Charity?"

She pressed her lips together until they almost disappeared. "Why are you being such an ass? *Charity*, really? Come on."

"You're out there and I'm not." Her fingers burned my wrist while I tried to make her understand. I couldn't see why she didn't get it, unless she didn't want to get it. "You're having a life." Now she was spending all day around real guys, guys who were not mental patients, who didn't obsess about killing themselves, who had never embarrassed themselves in Group.

"Stop acting like I'm up on some pedestal. Anyway, you're going to be out soon yourself. Don't you know that?"

I snickered.

"I'm serious, Ryan. You went from hiding under your bed to helping some of the new kids. You and Jake used to go on and on about dying, and now you talk about catching up in school. You used to walk around like a zombie, off in your own little world. Now, most of the time, you manage to stay here with the rest of us." Her fingers tightened. "Even though you've been acting like a jerk all night, you're still here. I could tell you were angry. So you're angry; at least you're something. You're not *nothing* anymore."

She let go and I had the wild urge to grab her back, to hang on to her as if she could keep me alive. But I didn't. I let her go, and when she called me two days later, I was able to tell her that she was right. They were getting ready to let me out, too.

The truth was that when she touched me, it stirred something that had been dead in me for months. The whole idea of girls and sex had burned out, gone to ashes, drifted under layers of black sludge. I'd stopped daydreaming about that or hoping for it or even remembering it existed. I'd forgotten what it was like to want that, forgotten how it felt to trace a girl's body with my eyes and want to trace it with my hands. I'd been numb until Val's fingers on the thin skin of my wrist reminded me of that heat, jolted me back into that hunger.

SIX

Nicki wanted to go to the waterfall as soon as we got back from Seaton. I hadn't thought about what a hike it was from her house, a much longer way than from mine, and all uphill. We were both panting when we reached the pool. Some little kids were plunking rocks in the water, but they ran away when they saw us coming.

I stripped off my T-shirt. Nicki pulled off hers, too, dropped it on the bank, and plunged into the water. I watched her for a minute, her bra dark blue against the paleness of her back, until she disappeared under the curtain of water. I didn't know what she meant by tearing off her shirt in front of me: that she didn't care if I saw her that way, because I was nobody? Or that she was so upset by what had happened with Andrea that she didn't know what she was doing?

She came out a minute later, gasping, water streaming from her hair. "Did you see this place last spring?" she said. "The water would knock you over, if you were stupid enough to stand under it."

I already knew this, because I had been stupid enough.

Without answering, I waded in and ducked under the fall, willing it to wash away the china figurines, the bland smile, the rattling air conditioner, and every trace of the great failure of Psychic Andrea. The water hammered down on me and I stood there longer than I'd ever managed before, realizing that Nicki was right: the dryness of August had cut the power of the cascade a little. But when I pulled out, its roaring still filled my head.

"I was getting ready to go in after you," Nicki said, rubbing her arms. I handed her my T-shirt to dry off with, then put it on damp. She wriggled into her dry shirt and squeezed her hair out over the moss.

"Are you okay?" I asked her.

"No."

We went to my place. The basement workout room had a closet full of Mom's gym clothes, and I gave Nicki a pair of exercise pants to wear while we spread her shorts on the deck railing. I dumped my wet clothes in the washer so Mom wouldn't see them.

My parents knew I swam in the stream, but they didn't know I stood under the waterfall. When we'd first moved here, they'd told me the waterfall was dangerous, but they had never forbidden me to go under it—I guess because it never occurred to them that I would. I didn't plan to tell them, either, and the fewer chances they had to see my wet clothes, the fewer questions they would ever think to ask.

Nicki and I sat on the living-room floor with the sunlight, filtered through evergreen needles, shining in on us.

"Don't take this the wrong way," Nicki said, "but I don't see why somebody who lives in a place like this would want to kill himself." She glanced at me, but I stared out the window. She probably didn't realize I'd heard that one, or variations on it, a hundred times before—and that I'd even said it to myself. I often thought I had nothing to complain about, compared to some of the stories I'd heard at Patterson. There were kids who'd been raped by their own parents, kids who'd been beaten or burned or choked, kids whose brains were so fucked up by drugs that I didn't know how they managed to feed themselves. There were kids who never knew which parent they'd be staying with on any given day, or when they'd be traded for a chunk of money in some divorce fight. Knowing all those stories confused me more, because I didn't have any of that going on. So I didn't know why the hell I kept falling into the pit, why I could never see what was pushing me down there.

Nicki and I sat awhile longer. At one point I got up and brought in a bowl of nuts and sunflower seeds and cranberries. We gorged on it, licking the salt off our fingers.

"This isn't—bird food, is it?" she said once, pausing in mid-crunch.

I laughed. "What if I said yes, now that we've eaten half the bowl?"

She squeaked.

"No," I said, grinning at her, and she swallowed. "It's just this healthy-snack crap my mother likes to buy. Anyway, I'm eating it, too, right?"

"Yeah, but you have a death wish."

I laughed again. Her face had frozen the second after she said it, as if she wanted to bite the words right out of the air and take them back into her mouth. But I was okay. In fact, I wished more kids at school would say things like that to me, instead of sneaking glances from twenty feet away like they usually did. Not that I knew how to let them know it was okay.

I couldn't stop thinking about the session at Andrea's, the weird *waiting* while we'd tried to contact Nicki's father. "What was your dad like?" I asked. I lay on the couch, while she sat on the floor scooping up the last nuts and berries.

She stopped with her fingers in her mouth and stared at me. Then she pulled her hand free and said, "I had this doll that used to be Kent's. Well, it was a boy doll; Kent called it an action figure. I named him Slade because I thought it was the coolest name ever." She ran her fingers along the bottom of the bowl, coating them with salt. "One day I left Slade down in Seaton Park, and I didn't realize it till we got home. I was hysterical. Matt and Kent told me he would get stolen or rained on or chewed up by wild animals. And my dad drove down to the park to get him, even though dinner was ready. That's the kind of person Dad was." She put her fingers in her mouth again, to suck off the salt. I watched her lips.

She seemed to be waiting for me to speak, but when I didn't, she took her hand out of her mouth and shook it, drying it in the air. "He used to bet on the horses at Sandford, and sometimes he took me. I love seeing the horses run, especially when they run right past where you're standing, like thunder. We used to plan what we'd do with the money he won, except he hardly ever won any. Once he won, like, a hundred bucks and we had a big dinner and I ordered crème brûlée for dessert." She laughed. "I didn't even know what it was. I called it 'cream brooley.'"

I rested my chin on my hands. "What else?" I felt a little like Dr. Briggs. It was nice to be the listener for once, not to have to scrape things out of my own brain to talk about.

"He used to fight with my mom. About money, and how late he stayed out with his buddies." She tried to spin the bowl, but it didn't work well on the carpet. "He never talked about suicide. As far as I know."

I'd never talked about it, either—at least, not beforehand.

She looked up at me. "He shot himself in the woods behind the house. My brother Matt and I found him."

My stomach jumped. I squashed down mental images of blood and brains, shattered bone. I could not imagine how horrible that would be, to find anyone who'd shot himself, let alone your own father. Especially since she'd also seen that kid drown at the waterfall. God, how had she made it to fifteen without her mind cracking, without ending up at a place like Patterson? "That sucks. I'm sorry, Nicki."

"Easy for you to say. Who would've found *you*?"

"We're not talking about me."

"I just want to know why he did it." She held her eyes steady on mine. "Why did *you* do it? And don't tell me you're not my dad. I don't care. He's not here to ask, and you are."

"You should ask your mom," I said. "After all—I didn't know your dad, and she did."

"She can't talk about him. If the subject ever gets *near* to coming up, she gets this sick look on her face. And anyway, you do know him. I mean, you know what it's like to feel the way he felt."

"It's not the same for everyone," I said. "In my Group, at the hospital, everybody's stories were different."

"That's not what I mean. I want to know how you get to the point where—killing yourself is something you can take seriously. Where you think, 'Yeah, I can do that.'"

I closed my eyes so I wouldn't have to look at her anymore.

"Tell me," she said.

Maybe I wouldn't have told her if we hadn't gone together to Andrea's house. If I hadn't tried to help Andrea conjure up the ghost of Nicki's father, if I hadn't seen Nicki cry, if she hadn't just joked with me as if I were a normal person instead of some fragile unbalanced psycho. If she hadn't been the one to find her father.

But all those things had happened. So I took a breath and began to talk.

We moved into this house, my mother's dream house, halfway through my sophomore year. I'd never been the new kid in school before. I hadn't realized how weird it would be when you can't even find the bathrooms—never mind figuring out the "right" tables in the cafeteria and the "right" seats on the bus. When you're new, you're really alone.

And then the house started leaking.

It happened during the storms of February, when a weird thaw hit us with warm rains. Water poured down, gushed over the gutters, and pounded on the roof.

It also dribbled into the house.

The edges of the windows leaked. The roof leaked. One night, lightning flashed like a strobe while we ran around the house spreading pots to catch the rainwater. I laughed because this fancy house, my mother's obsession for years, had been slapped together so sloppily that it literally leaked at the seams.

"I don't see anything funny," my mother snapped, dropping towels to absorb the water that had already puddled on the floors and soaked the carpet.

"It's crazy," I managed to say, catching my breath. I couldn't believe she didn't see a little bit of irony or gallows humor or whatever in the situation. Here we were running around like maniacs, trying to catch each new mini-waterfall as it sprang to life. I was in my shorts, since that's what I wore to bed. My parents wore robes over their pajamas, and their hair stuck out all over their heads, and we kept tripping as we raced from one leak to another.

The house was supposed to be perfect, and it wasn't. Something about that made me feel better than I'd felt in weeks, eased the pressure on my chest. It had been a long time since I'd laughed and it would be a long time until I laughed again, but that night I couldn't stop.

We rented a house in Seaton while this house got reroofed and recaulked and whatever else they had to do to seal it up. My mother was furious, documenting every step for the lawsuit she eventually filed against the builder. We lived out of boxes and suitcases, with most of our own furniture left up here under plastic tarps. Everything in the rented house was strange. I bumped into walls when I went to the bathroom in the middle of the night. Nothing belonged to me.

Since Seaton High was still pretty new to me, too, I didn't fit anywhere. I stumbled through the days always a little lost, a little behind. Because I didn't know the team schedules, I missed baseball tryouts. When I talked to the coach, he agreed to let me come to practice and show him what I could do. But before I made it, I got the worst sore throat of my life, with chills and fever.

It turned out I had mono, and I was so sick I could just about crawl to the bathroom. I used to stop at a certain spot midway down the hall, where my mother had plugged in a nightlight shaped like a scallop shell. I would lie there with my face against the carpet, inhaling crumbs and dirt specks the vacuum had missed, staring at the plastic shell and gathering my strength to make the second half of the trip. Mostly that's what I remember from two weeks of sickness: that nightlight.

The coach sent me a message to forget about baseball. He said I was only a sophomore anyway and could try out next year, but I found it hard to believe I would ever play again. I'd also had to stop running—the running I'd done for fun, not for a team. I never tracked my times or distances but did it because I liked it, because it sent the blood racing through me and made me feel less like I was living behind a pane of glass.

■ ■ ■ ■ ■

"What do you mean by a pane of glass?" Nicki asked.

"It's like I can see and hear everyone, but I'm not really there with them. It comes and goes—I mean, it always did. Until last year, when it stuck around."

Dr. Briggs once asked me how long I'd felt it. I thought maybe it started when I was eight, the first time I went off the high dive at my swim class. Nobody else had acted scared of the diving board, so I marched right off it like it was nothing. I only got the shakes afterward, in the locker room.

"There's a numbness that goes with it," I told Nicki. "It's like being dead but not officially dead. I mean, that's the way I always thought of it."

She nodded as if that made some kind of sense, touching my hand. I forced myself to look through her, to keep talking, because if I stopped and let myself feel her hand on my skin, I was never going to get through the part about the garage.

This hollow numbness seemed to go on forever. My mother was obsessed with the house. The contractors kept stopping work on the roof and windows for no reason, disappearing for days and leaving things half done, tarps flapping in the wind. My father went on the road, came back, and said, "They're not done *yet*?"

It never seemed to stop raining. I had no friends at school. I was over the mono—at least I could go to classes again—but I couldn't run. I came home from school every day and went to bed.

There's nothing like mono exhaustion. It's not like being tired after a good workout or missing a night of sleep. With those kinds of tired, you're spent, but as soon as you stop moving, you start filling back up. With mono, you don't recharge. You feel like you never had energy and never will. This would be scary, except it takes energy to care and you don't have energy.

I didn't know how to change things. All I knew was that everything felt wrong, and I felt wrong, like I shouldn't even exist. I hated getting up in the morning. I hated slogging through the motions at school. I hated my mother's anxious nagging and my father's disappearing. I hated having nothing to look forward to, ever.

Our rented house had a garage. One night I went down to start my mother's car. She had gone to bed; my father was out at a late meeting. I didn't have a license or anything, but I knew how to start an engine. I rolled down the car windows and left the garage door closed. I had heard that in just a few minutes you could fill a garage with fumes strong enough to kill. I turned the key and let the engine chug for a minute, maybe less.

I turned it off because I suddenly remembered something else I'd heard, about the fumes getting into the house, too, and killing people there. I got out of the car, found a sheet that someone had used as a drop cloth, and spread it along the crack under the door that led from the garage to the house.

I got back into the car, but this time I couldn't turn the key. What if the sheet wasn't enough? It was just cotton, probably not gas-tight. What if the fumes got through? What if I killed my mother?

And did I really want to do this to myself?

I couldn't think of anything else I wanted to do, any way that life was going to get better, any way this dead blackness was going to leave, but at the same time turning the key seemed like a lot of trouble.

I sat there arguing with myself, my hand on the key but not turning it. I sat there and sat there and sat there.

Finally the garage door rumbled open, and my father drove in. He got out of his own car and began to cross in front of my mother's. "What the hell are you doing?" he said when he saw me. "You don't have a license, mister. What are you doing in that car?"

I just blinked at him. He thought I was getting ready for a joyride. He might've gone on thinking that if he hadn't seen the sheet under the door. When he saw it, his head swung back to me, took in the open window, the sight of me in the driver's seat. His eyes flicked back to the garage door, which had been closed until he opened it.

Nicki squeezed my hand, crunched down on it, and I almost stopped speaking. But having come this far, I figured I might as well go the rest of the way. Tell everything.

"Did you start this car?" my dad said. "Don't you know you can't run a car in a closed space?"

"Yeah," I said. "I know that." It was the closest I could come to telling him the truth. We stared at each other. I think he was waiting for me to tell him I wasn't trying to do what we both knew I was trying to do.

"Did you run the engine?"

"Only for a minute," I said.

"Where the hell is your mother?"

I pointed at the door to the house.

"Get out of the car."

But I couldn't move. I put my head down on the steering wheel and he ran inside, calling for my mother.

"I wonder if my dad put his hand on the trigger first without pulling it," Nicki whispered. "If he started to and stopped, you know."

I didn't know. But if I had to bet, I would bet yes. He may have sat there with his finger on the trigger as long as I sat in that stupid garage with my hand on the key.

My father took me to the emergency room, where they checked me out for carbon-monoxide poisoning. Which, of course, I didn't have. But the nurse asked me if I had tried to hurt myself.

"Yes," I said. "But I'm not very good at it."

My own words struck me as hilarious, the funniest thing I'd heard since the night we ran around trying to plug up our leaking house, but the nurse didn't laugh. She called for other people to talk to me. They asked me more questions like that and then they told my father I couldn't go home because I was a danger to myself.

"I don't feel dangerous," I told someone, a nurse or intern or whoever it was. But they checked me in anyway.

I told the psych resident who saw me the next day that I hadn't even really done anything; I had only turned the key for a minute. She told me my parents had searched my room at home and found ten bottles of painkillers, way more than I would need for any headache, and way more than I would need to kill myself. She asked me why I had it.

I knew the medicine could kill me. I'd bought it because it made me feel better every time I bought a new bottle. A little better, for a little while. But I hadn't used the bottles because I knew an overdose would destroy my liver, and if I failed I didn't want to be alive with a screwed-up liver.

Not that I told the psych resident any of that. She asked me why I had all that medicine and I said I kept forgetting I already had it, and buying a new bottle. She asked why it had been hidden under the bed. I said it wasn't hidden; that was just where I wanted to keep it. She managed not to roll her eyes.

Later that day, after my parents had telephoned God knows how many hospitals and the insurance company, they found a place for me at Patterson, which was only an hour outside of Seaton.

"We're lucky they have such a good facility for adolescents right here," my mother said as we waited in the hospital lobby for my father to bring the car around, so they could drive me over there.

"Yeah," I said. "We're lucky to have so many screwed-up teenagers close by."

She whirled on me, her hand raised. Neither of my parents

had hit me since I was about five, when they used to give me a swat on the butt for such crimes as drawing on the walls with ketchup. I closed my eyes, waiting for the slap, but it didn't come.

She didn't say a word. When I opened my eyes, she was no longer facing me. She stared at a vending machine, at candy bars trapped behind glass and coiled wire, gripping her purse with both hands. She was quiet when my father pulled up, quiet while we got into the car and drove out on the highway. Then she burst into tears and bent over in the front seat—wailing, smearing her lipstick and black eye makeup on her hands and sleeve.

"Melissa, don't; it'll be okay," my father said, one hand darting over to pat her shoulder. His head swiveled, checking the lanes around us. He tried to pull the car over to the right, but nobody would let him over. They sped past, punching their horns whenever our car edged into the next lane.

"Damn it," he said, as another one blared at us. "Help me here. Watch your side of the car and tell me when it's clear." His voice rose. "Melissa. I need you to do this."

She sobbed and the car kept going forward at sixty-five miles an hour, forward because nobody would let us stop.

"Can you keep yourself together for a few minutes?"

"I'm trying."

"Can you please—"

"Forget it!" She straightened her back, black streaks shining on her cheeks. "Nobody's going to let you over. Nobody gives a damn. Our heads could be on fire, and nobody would slow down for half a minute to let us get off the road. Just keep driving, Harry."

"If you need to stop—"

"I don't. I'm fine." She stared out the windshield, the wet smears drying on her face. "Keep going."

I watched them and knew I should feel something, but I felt nothing except the old hopelessness. Which I had no right to feel, because I was a healthy kid from a good family. A kid whose mother wouldn't even slap him when he was stabbing her, a kid whose parents were bleeding money to send him to a place like Patterson.

"When you knew you were in trouble—why didn't you talk to anybody?" Nicki asked.

"Like who?"

"Your parents?"

"What was I gonna say? That I felt like I was behind glass? That would've made a lot of sense."

"If you told them you were thinking about killing yourself, I'm sure they would've been interested."

Her voice was full of common sense. I buried my face in my arms and breathed in. The couch smelled faintly like roses; the cleaning woman sprayed something on it every week that would probably give us cancer years from now.

In spite of the sickly fabric-cleaner smell, I breathed in deep and slow, trying to hold off panic, the shudders that wanted to roll through me. I should've known what it would do to me to tell Nicki, how raw I would feel. The last time I'd told this story Val and Jake had had to glue me back together. I wasn't at Patterson anymore; I couldn't afford to break myself open like this. Why had I thought I could help Nicki, anyway?

Nicki rested her hand on my back. "Are you okay?"

"Yes."

"Seriously."

I turned my head so she could see my face. "Yes."

"I'm sorry I made you tell me that."

"You didn't make me."

She frowned at the wall. "I've been pushing you to tell me."

"Did it help?"

"What do you mean?"

"Did you get what you wanted?" I said.

"I—I don't know."

We stared at each other, the pupils small in her gray eyes, small in the light from the windows.

Nicki and I ended up outside, tossing a baseball back and forth. One of my old gloves fit her. The sky had paled to a nothing color, the dirty white of old socks. I wasn't sure how we decided to start playing catch except that we needed a break, needed to pull back from what we'd said to each other.

Nicki's aim was okay, but her technique sucked. "Like this," I told her, demonstrating. "No—bring your arm back like—are you watching?"

She giggled and tried to balance the ball on her foot. "You don't have to turn this into a lesson, Coach."

I shut up about her throwing. My parents used to do that—try to turn every blasted thing into a "learning experience."

"Unless you want me to give you volleyball lessons next," she went on.

"Volleyball?"

"Yeah, I was the setter on my team last year. I bet I make varsity this fall, even though I'll just be a sophomore."

The word "varsity" jabbed me in the stomach. I wondered whether I could've made the baseball team if I hadn't been sick. And whether I would be able to play next spring, after missing a year. But all I said to Nicki was, "Come on, throw the ball."

The sky darkened, but the air didn't cool off. "It's so hot," Nicki said as the ball went back and forth between us, smacking into our gloves. "If we keep this up, I'll have to go back to the waterfall."

"Okay with me."

"It's true what they say about you." She laughed. "You do practically live up there."

My throw went a little wild; she lurched to catch it. "Who says what about me?"

Her face flushed. "It's just—people know you like to hang out up there. They've seen you. That's how I knew where to find you."

She sent the ball back to me. I caught and held it. It had never occurred to me that she'd hunted for me on purpose. I'd always thought our meeting there had been an accident. "You came looking for me?"

"Well, yeah." She scratched her arm, staring at my knees instead of my face. "I went up to the waterfall all the time anyway. A couple of times, people said you'd just left when I got there, so I started going earlier. I wanted to talk to you about my dad. Didn't you know that?"

"I never thought about it," I said slowly. "I figured I just reminded you of your dad; I didn't know you came looking for me."

"Well, we talked about him anyway, so what's the difference?" She raised her eyes, met mine for a second. "Are you going to throw the ball?"

"No difference," I said, but it did make a difference, and it made my stomach burn that I couldn't figure out what the hell the difference was.

"Throw the ball," she said.

I stood there, my mouth drying by the second, the glove hiding the ball in my hand. "So you only used me for my suicide stories, but hey, I knew that all along, right?"

Nicki shook her head. "That's not it."

Clouds pushed down on the tops of the trees. Pressure built above me, inside me. I tasted panic. I told myself there was nothing to panic about, but I tasted it anyway.

I hurled the ball. Her hand snapped up, and the ball thwacked into her glove. She pulled her hand out of the glove and shook it. "What, are you trying to knock my fingers off?"

"What else do people say about me?"

"Nothing." She wiggled her fingers.

"Are you going to tell them all about me now? My lame-ass night in the garage, and how I couldn't even turn the key?"

She walked up to me, and I took one step back. I couldn't stand her being so close, couldn't believe I'd let her rest her hand on my skin earlier. The heavy humid air filled my throat, made it hard to breathe.

"What is your problem?" she said.

"I don't like people knowing shit about me."

Wind stirred the treetops, not yet reaching us on the ground. She stretched a hand toward me. I smelled my own sweat and couldn't understand why she didn't gag from the stink of it. Her fingertips brushed my arm, and I flinched away.

"Don't touch me."

"Ryan, you're acting like an idiot. Listen to me."

"I *am* an idiot, for telling you all that shit." I needed a good dousing in the waterfall. I needed the roar, the smack in the face when I tilted my head upward into the spray. "Why don't you go have a laugh with your friends? Tell them how I hang around the waterfall, and how I didn't have the guts to turn the key."

"Ryan—"

"And how I talk too much to the wrong fucking people."

She froze.

"Go on. Get out of here; it's going to rain any minute."

Cold wind rushed through the trees. Her drying shorts blew off the deck railing. The low plants growing around our house, the ferns and bushes, bowed and touched the ground. Nicki eyed the sky.

"We are *not* done here," she said. She tossed the ball and glove on the ground and grabbed her shorts. She ran into the woods, into the dimness of the coming storm.

SEVEN

A few minutes after Nicki left, fat raindrops began to splat down. I went inside and raised the kitchen windows to let in the smell of rain on hot ground. I opened the door to the deck, and wind poured in. It blew a magazine off the coffee table and knocked a vase from the kitchen counter. The vase broke but no water spilled, since Mom never put anything in it.

"Ryan!" My mother ran in and slammed everything shut. She never liked outside air, with its dirt and pollen; she preferred filtered air. "What on earth were you thinking?"

"I was cooling off the house."

"The air conditioning's on. What's the matter with you?"

Rain thundered down, hammered on the roof and the window glass, drummed on the deck. The living-room windows turned liquid.

Mom ran her finger around the edge of a windowpane, as she often did when it rained, testing for leaks. We hadn't had any problems since moving back in after the repairs, but she kept testing anyway. "What have you done with yourself all day?" she asked, with strained cheerfulness.

Let's see: stood under a waterfall, went to see a phony psychic, relived the worst night of my life, fought with Nicki. "Not much."

"You might say . . ." Her eyes searched my face. "You might say you haven't done much since you finished your schoolwork last month."

"It's vacation."

"Ryan," she said, taking the dustpan and broom out of the kitchen closet, "I think it's time you started doing things again. Your father and I have been very patient; we haven't kept you on a short leash. But—"

"'Leash'?" I said. "What am I, a dog?"

"I didn't mean that." She held out the broom and dustpan. "Come clean up this vase."

I swept up the fragments. "I'm not on a leash."

"That was a poor choice of words," she said. "My point is that you need structure. We didn't want to pressure you into taking on too much too soon, and we thought something like camp or a summer class might be too much, but now I wonder. I worry about you drifting, not having any goals—"

"I have goals."

"Such as?"

"I'm going to start running again." I dumped broken glass in the trash.

"That's very nice." Her tone dripped syrup. "But I'm thinking about more than just a hobby."

"Will you stop talking at me like I'm five years old? I was a mental patient, not a moron."

She sucked in her breath. "You like saying that, don't you?"

"Not really."

She gripped the kitchen counter where the vase had stood. "You like shocking me."

"Why should it shock you? That's what I was."

She shook her head. "You like saying it in the ugliest way possible. Dr. Briggs says it makes you feel that you're in control."

I hated when she talked like that, as if she were looking me up in a manual and reading a section titled "How to Respond When Ryan Reminds You He Was in the Nuthouse." I threw the broom and dustpan in the closet, instead of hanging them on their special little hooks.

"Ryan—" Her face creased, and I knew I needed to stop, to pull back, because it never took much to make her crumble. But my nerves were stretched tight, on the verge of snapping, and I wasn't sure if it was because of what she'd said, or if this tension was left over from my scene with Nicki. I only knew I needed her to shut up.

She didn't.

"You can't hold your illness over our heads for the rest of your life. It doesn't excuse you for rudeness. It doesn't—"

"You're the one holding it over my head."

Her face collapsed, and she stood sobbing in the middle of the kitchen. Guilt knifed through me. I opened the closet door and hung up the dustpan and broom. But she kept crying, with her hand at her face and her shoulders quivering.

I should've tried to hug her or at least touch her shoulder, but I couldn't. It was like watching someone drowning, and worrying that if you stuck your arm out to help them, they'd drag you under, too. I tapped the sides of my legs while she choked, tears pouring over her fingers. Finally I managed to pull a paper towel off the roll and hand it to her.

"Thank you," she murmured, blotting her face. "Why don't you just go upstairs." Her voice was calm now, thick from crying, and she wouldn't look at me.

In my room, I went right to the computer. Val wasn't around, but Jake was.

"What are you up to?" I asked him.

"The Mom wants me to go outside. I told her there's nothing out there I need to see. Then she gives me a guilt trip about mowing the lawn."

"Join us out here in the world where they have marvels like this." I sent him a picture of an eggplant whose owner claimed it looked like Albert Einstein. After all the drama with Nicki and Mom, it was a relief to focus on vegetables that supposedly resembled famous scientists. I could halfway understand why Jake never wanted to leave his room.

"See, I would go outside if they had eggplants like that in my yard, but it's just a bunch of boring GRASS that needs to be mowed," Jake wrote. "I don't know why the Magnificent One can't mow it. Just a touch from his golden fingers and the grass would probably mow itself."

"Hey, if your brother doesn't have an Einstein eggplant, he's not that magnificent."

Jake went silent then, for so long I thought he might've dropped off. I was about to check when he typed, "What's it like for you at school?"

"Not bad," I wrote, thinking of the way I floated through the halls like an iceberg, people steering around me. "Not great. Not bad."

"For me it's bad."

"How's that?"

Silence, the cursor blinking on my screen. Then Jake came back on.

"It was always bad last year. But now I hear EVERYONE knows I was at Patterson."

"Well, me too. They knew when I went back in May. So what?"

"What did they do to you?" he asked.

"Mostly they stayed away. Like I was carrying Suicide Plague."

"I wish they would stay away from me."

Before I could answer, he wrote: "The Mom's yelling at me to get off the computer. See ya."

I sat for a minute, wondering why Jake had asked me about school and what he meant by "bad." I could imagine fifty thousand shades of bad, fifty thousand ways that school could go wrong. Maybe Patterson should've given us all a special course in reentering the world. Not that I knew what they could've taught there. They tried to prepare us; they made a "transition plan" for each of us. But maybe there was no way to escape the weirdness, no way around the rumors and stares and sneers—no way except to live through it.

When my counselor at Patterson had told me I was leaving, the first thing I said was, "I'm not ready." Even though I'd always said I couldn't wait to get out of there.

"You are ready."

"But I'm not—I mean, I'm still—" I gave up and started a whole new sentence. "I thought I would feel a lot better than this by the time I left."

"You'll have to continue your medication, and I'm referring you to Elizabeth Briggs for therapy. But you don't need hospital care anymore. At this point you'll improve more when you're back home, living your life again."

Now I wondered if they'd told the same thing to Jake. Because sometimes "living your life" was the whole problem.

A message from Nicki popped up on my computer. Just what I needed.

"in case you're wondering i did NOT make it home before the rain. do you believe fake psychic called & said she'd received a message for me from my dad? i didn't believe her but i had to know what it was. i'm such a sucker. it was some bull about making the most of life & being happy, blah, anyone could've made that up. you didn't do much better when we were at her house & you were trying to channel my dad but at least i give you credit for trying."

I didn't answer her. I thought of her alone, drenched by rain, calling that psychic. Calling, probably, before she'd even dried off. Holding her breath just in case Andrea had something meaningful to say—and the thunk in her stomach when she realized that it was another false alarm. But even thinking of all that, I couldn't make myself reply to her. I couldn't get past the burning in my throat, the wall that had come up between us.

"Ryan i guess you are still mad at me but i don't care. go ahead be mad all you want. what do i care."

I didn't answer that one, either.

"by the way i'm glad you didn't kill yourself. now go ahead & go back to being mad at me, i'm kind of mad at you too now."

Or that one.

I opened the closet, took down the package, and unfolded the paper bag. The draw to touch this bundle was always there, but now it filled my brain, and I wouldn't be able to relax or think about anything else until I got this over with.

I stuck my hand in and rubbed the pink fabric of the sweater. It had been soft the first time I touched it, but it was rough now, as if I could feel every fiber and thread.

The roughness jolted me out of whatever trance I'd been in. I wrapped up the sweater and thrust it back on the shelf, pissed that I'd gotten sucked into touching it again. Guilt like concrete filled my stomach, my chest, even the inside of my head.

EIGHT

That night my father came home for dinner. He was a sales-
man, but not the kind that knocks on doors or works in a store.
He sold industrial equipment to factories. His passport had stamps
from all over the world. When I was little, I made myself a passport
like his, with hand-drawn stamps from made-up places. I didn't
realize until I was in second grade that not everyone did this, that
the other kids thought it was strange to play with fake passports
and old baggage-claim stickers.

Dad kept promising to take me with him, but whenever I
asked about a specific trip, he'd say, "I'm booked solid with meet-
ings. I wouldn't have any time for you." I'd told him I could sightsee
on my own—I saw myself running through the streets of foreign
cities, bouncing along in a river of languages I didn't understand,
free—but neither of my parents liked that idea.

When we all sat down to eat, my mother gave me a quivery
smile, so I guessed I was forgiven for breaking the vase earlier. She

divided her fish into equal sections, never letting it touch her carrots or green beans.

"There's a game on tonight," Dad told me. "Want to watch?"

"Okay." I never knew if he did these father-son nights out of obligation or because he wanted to, but I didn't mind. It wasn't like I had other plans.

Mom went upstairs to watch something else because she said baseball was maddeningly slow, and we settled on the living-room couch. The way baseball announcers talk is very relaxing. It's like they have nothing to do with the rest of their lives besides watch whatever game is in front of them. Not that I listened to every word. I just liked the sound of it, the stream of facts and numbers and stats and names. It pushed everything else out of my mind.

"Your mother mentioned that you want to start running again," Dad said during a commercial.

"Oh—yeah—I did say that."

He paused before he spoke again. For the past few months, he always seemed to digest my words, weigh and analyze them. Or maybe he was weighing his own words, trying not to set me off on another trip to Crazytown. "Don't forget, the treadmill is downstairs, anytime you want to use it."

"I know. But I want to try the trails around here." The treadmill had become my mother's thing. I no longer wanted to run indoors. I'd been walled in, cushioned, since coming out of Patterson, and now I wanted to push myself again. To find the edges of things.

"Good for you," Dad said, a little too heartily. I wondered if either of my parents would ever completely relax around me again.

▪ ▪ ▪ ▪ ▪

I had come home from Patterson to this house; the contractors had finished sealing it up while I was in the hospital. I would never go back to the house with the garage, or the room where my parents had found pills under my bed.

My bed looked strange, my computer and desk as if they belonged to someone I'd known years ago. The first thing I did was hang up Val's painting, and then I felt a little better. Mom hovered, frowning. "What's that? Did you paint that? Oh, Val did? Isn't that . . . interesting. Do you want anything to eat? Or drink? I have some fruit, and crackers—I could make you a sandwich—do you need to take a nap?"

"I thought I would take a walk," I said, itching to be outside, with no walls or fences.

"A walk? Where?"

"Out in the woods."

"Alone? A walk to where? Why?"

"Just around. To get some exercise. Nowhere special."

She'd insisted on coming with me. I had to wait for her to find a sweater, and good walking shoes, and the house keys, and finally we set out. I wanted to be alone, but I knew I shouldn't push it when I'd barely come in the door. For all she knew, I was planning to off myself in the forest.

"I'm okay, Mom," I told her as we walked. I wasn't completely okay. But I wasn't on the verge of suicide, which was the part she needed to know.

She tried to laugh, an *I'm not worried* lie. "I know, but—"

I bent to pick up a pinecone. She eyed it in my hands as if it were a clue, a sign of where I stood on the crazy/sane meter. I turned the cone, studying its spiral shape, and tossed it back into the woods.

We'd barely left the house behind when she said, "How much farther are you going to walk?"

"I don't know."

"We shouldn't go too far."

"We just got started. I need some exercise."

"But, Ryan, you have a whole workout room in the basement."

"I want to be outside. I've been cooped up forever."

"Well, we've *been* outside."

"Only for ten minutes!"

"Please don't fight me on this," she said, and I let her turn us around. I would get my time alone, I told myself. It would just take longer than I'd expected.

Since that day, my parents had loosened their grip on me, but only by inches. During the commercials in the baseball game, my father looked over at me like he wanted to say something, but whatever it was, he didn't say it.

Before I went to bed, I rooted around the bottom of my closet until I found the trail runners Dad had gotten me at the beginning of the summer. I'd told him back in June that I was thinking of running again, and he'd driven me into Seaton to get the shoes. "It's good to see you taking an interest in things again," he'd said, hanging over me in the store while I'd laced them up, beaming as if

I'd brought home an Olympic medal. But I hadn't used the shoes; buying them had been a big enough step.

Now I pulled them out of the box, out of the tissue paper, and set them on the floor next to my bed. They smelled of rubber and new plastic. They smelled like the beginning of something.

Val was online, answering a message I'd left her earlier. "You rang, sir?"

I typed back: "Yeah. I had a shitty day. I said several shitty things to people & I'm not even sure why."

"Like who?"

"You know that girl I told you about? She wanted to hear my whole garage story."

"Did you tell her?"

"Yup."

"You must be getting pretty close if you're telling her about the garage."

"It was because she told me all this stuff about her father. Next thing I knew I was telling her." I paused, then typed more: "The weird thing is, when you think about it, I never went that far in the garage. Remember how Alex always said it shouldn't even count as a real attempt? That I didn't try to kill myself, I tried to try?"

"What is this, a competition? Who's more serious about offing himself? The winner ends up in a box. Some victory!"

"I don't know."

"Alex was always trying to prove he was more fucked up than

anyone else. Like he would get some prize for being the worst one. I think he was jealous of you," Val wrote.

"What for?"

"Because you worked hard. And you knew how to listen to people, which he never did."

"No, if he was jealous it was because I had you and Jake."

"He was jealous because I never painted his portrait."

I laughed at that. Val had painted a lot at Patterson, but one thing she'd done for fun was "abstract portraits" of Jake and me, using finger paint. Jake was a bunch of skinny black lines. I was a blue cloud with orange and purple flashes. The whole thing was kind of a joke—when Jake saw his, he said, "I think of myself more as a green triangle." It made us laugh, even when nobody else did. That was the thing about Val and Jake and me: we had our own world, our own language.

"You could've cured Alex, turned his whole life around," I wrote now. "If only you'd painted him, too."

The cursor blinked at me. I could almost feel Val on the other end of this conversation, listening. Well, reading, but it was like listening.

"I miss you," she wrote. "I miss having conversations like this."

"Me too."

"I wrote a song. Can I send it to you?"

"Yes."

"Play it now, OK?"

"Yes. Send it."

She sent me the link to the music file, and I played it. It was a stormy instrumental: a piano and a guitar, with a few bursts of flute. I liked its roughness, and the way the flute kept surprising me. I typed, "WOW."

"You like?"

"It's incredible. Which instrument did you play?"

"Piano and flute. My brother did the guitar."

We wrote back and forth about the song, about how long she took to write it and how she recorded it and what her brother said about it. I didn't want to let her go; I was dreading the moment when our connection would break.

Back at Patterson I sometimes used to think—when I wasn't busy plotting my own obliteration, or trying to stop plotting it— that Val might like me. Nothing had happened between us in the hospital. Nothing except the spark when she circled my wrist with her hand. Now that we were out, I sometimes thought I should take a chance and tell her what I wanted. I might've done it already if she didn't live so far away.

And what if she wasn't interested? It would wreck what we had, and I'd end up with nothing. I couldn't help remembering what had happened with Amy Trillis—even though Val was nothing like Amy. So tonight, again, I signed off without saying anything to Val.

Looking back now, I'm not sure why I ever liked Amy Trillis. I fell hard at the beginning of sophomore year: my head full of her, my pulse jumping every time we were in the same room. I didn't talk to her, but everyone knew who she was. She was a junior, class vice president, a star on the girls' soccer team, one of the editors of the student Web page. She always seemed to know exactly who she was.

I liked her laugh, too. There was something warm about it, something that made me want to curl myself around her.

We had the same history class. She sat in front of me and one row to the right, perfect for me to watch her without being too obvious about it. She used a sparkly green pen, and she was always chewing on the cap. Sometimes her black curls fell down the left side of her face and I couldn't see her expression. My eyes would follow the curve of her shoulder and the line of her sweater. She didn't wear low-cut shirts or anything that was painted-on tight, but you could see her body. Everything she wore fit her, outlined her.

I watched her, but I didn't have the nerve to talk to her. Watching her was like watching someone on TV, that's how far away she seemed.

One day we were both absent when people had to pair up for group projects. The teacher caught me in homeroom the next day and told me Amy and I were the only two left, so I found Amy in the hall before class. I'd rehearsed what to say, because it was the first time I'd ever spoken directly to her. "Mrs. Bruno says we should work together on this project. Everyone else already has partners."

Amy took a step back, looked me up and down as if I had mold sprouting from my pores, and said, "No thanks."

Her two best friends, the girls who trailed her through the halls, giggled. My face began to heat up.

"We're the only two left," I said. It wasn't like I was asking her to have my children. This was a history project. An *assignment*.

She tossed her head. "I'll switch with somebody." Turning, she gripped the arm of her nearest friend, and all three of them burst into laughter. That laugh hit me right in the stomach. "God, he's the creepy guy who's always staring at me in class," Amy said, without bothering to lower her voice. Heat flashed over me, and I seemed to have a swarm of bees inside my head, a roaring buzz that almost—but not quite—drowned out the girls' giggling. They walked away, laughing so hard they staggered and bumped into one another. I went to my locker, sweat thick on my skin, feeling like everyone in school must've heard what had happened. The words she'd said played over and over in my head, drawing blood each time, cutting into my nerves.

And then the pane of glass came up, and the world seemed to move one step back from me, so at least I could breathe again.

In history, Martin Reyes came up and told me he'd switched with Amy so Amy could work with Dave Shaw. I said fine, I didn't care. I didn't look in Amy's direction—not then, and not ever again in that class. I hated when the teacher stood on the right side of the room, where Amy would've been in my line of sight. I refused to look in that direction, so Mrs. Bruno accused me of not paying attention.

Moving out of West Seaton, away from Amy Trillis, was a relief. But the shame about everything to do with her lived in the bottom of my stomach. I never really left any of it behind.

NINE

The morning after Nicki and I went to the psychic, I ran on the trails through the woods, splattering mud and skidding on slippery tree roots. Early as it was, steam was already filling the forest, dew dripping from the branches of pines and hemlocks. I hadn't run since the winter and I was in crappy shape; running pounded the breath out of me. But I didn't mind. I liked the blood roaring through my veins. I even liked sweating.

I followed the trail up and away from the waterfall, to the rim of an old quarry. There the path died and left me looking down a cliff wall, at scooped-out rock and dusty rubble on the ground below.

I walked the lip of the quarry, legs shaking, sweat streaming down my back. The vertical rock face stretched far beneath my feet. I kicked a rock out over the rim and watched it bounce in the dust below, remembering the day when I'd told Val I wished I could fly.

Someone had once strung a wire fence here, but it had rusted and sagged. The wires had curled and sprung free, and the fence no longer went all the way across. I wrapped my hand around the rusty wire.

Nicki's latest messages seeped through my brain. I didn't know how she managed to do that, to invade my head with her whispery lowercase letters, but I couldn't get rid of her. I kept hearing, "i'm glad you didn't kill yourself . . . i'm kind of mad at you too now . . ."

I wanted to help her, but I didn't know how. She always seemed to think I knew more than I did, that I was hiding the one secret she needed to learn.

I had secrets, but they had nothing to do with Nicki's father.

I held the loose wire, wanting to lean over the edge. I did lean forward, then pulled myself back. Something about heights pulled on me like a vortex. It wasn't a death wish, though. Every cell in my body breathed and pulsed, the opposite of the numbness that had sent me to Patterson.

I kicked another rock off the edge.

I wasn't done with Nicki yet, I knew. Maybe I couldn't give her the answers she wanted, but we weren't finished with each other.

I passed the waterfall on the way back, but Nicki wasn't there. I showered at home and walked down to her house, my legs trembling on the steep downhill.

Kent sat in the driveway, smoking—cigarettes this time. "Nicki here?" I asked him.

His eyebrows rose. "What's up with you two?"

"I just need to talk to her."

"Well, like I said, be careful with her." He stared at my wet hair. "You been under that fucking waterfall again?"

"Not today." I didn't get why it bothered him so much, unless maybe he thought it set a bad example for Nicki. "Why do you care?"

He shrugged. "I don't. Knock your brains loose if you want." He blew out a huge cloud of smoke, which I thought was a pretty ironic thing to do while giving me a safety lecture. Then he jerked his head toward the house. "Nicki's up in her room."

I picked my way over an empty motor-oil container, a pile of stones, and a broken rake and knocked at the front door. Kent said, "Just go in. Nobody else is home. She's upstairs."

I felt weird opening the door and walking in like I belonged there, but Kent was watching me, so I did it. The living room had such a low ceiling that my throat closed up. The room was filled with couches and rugs and tables and magazines and tools and coffee cups and I don't know what else; I just had the impression of stuff crowding me, stealing the air. It smelled like pepper and cabbage and cinnamon, dog and gasoline and mildew. I realized why else the air was so heavy: they didn't have the air conditioning on or the windows open.

I headed straight up the stairs, which thudded hollowly under my feet. In the middle of each step, white fibers showed through the mud-colored carpet. I stopped at the top.

"Nicki!" I called.

She opened one of the doors along the hall. "What are you doing here?"

"I want to talk to you."

She stuck out one hip, and I thought she was about to tell me to go to hell, but then she pulled the door open wider and stepped back. I walked in. This room was even more crowded than downstairs: a bed piled with pillows and twisted sheets and more magazines; a dresser squeezed in between the end of the bed and the wall, its top smothered in nail-polish bottles, juice glasses, markers, batteries—

"What do you want?" Nicki plunked down on a stool in front of the dresser, which had a big mirror behind it. "The pants? They're in the wash."

I'd forgotten all about the pants Nicki had borrowed the day before. "Oh—no hurry." I sat on the bed behind her, and we met each other's eyes in the mirror. I was sitting on an open magazine, but I didn't want to move yet. I wanted to be steady, not squirming, when I said what I'd come to say.

"I'm sorry," I told her.

"For what?"

"That I didn't answer your messages yesterday."

She uncapped a bottle of nail polish. The smell filled the room. I liked it but figured it was probably bad for us, a chemical smell we shouldn't inhale too deeply. She took the tiny brush and swiped it down over a thumbnail: silver. "Why'd you get so— suspicious? What'd you think I was trying to do?"

I ran a hand through my hair, saw it sticking up in the mirror, and smoothed it back down. "I don't talk about this stuff with too many people, you know."

"I haven't told anybody what you've told me." She finished painting her thumbnail and blew on it. She capped the bottle and stared at her single silver nail. "I always planned to talk to you about my dad, but that doesn't mean I just want to—squeeze some information out of you and disappear." Nicki met my eyes in the mirror again, blowing on her thumbnail. "I like hanging out with you, and talking. My brothers and a lot of the kids at school don't think I'm smart enough to talk about anything that matters."

I believed her—though it was hard to see how anyone could make the mistake of underestimating Nicki.

"You must trust me a little, right?" she went on. "Since you're here?"

I did. It was something about the way she always seemed ready to burst through her skin, as if she couldn't hide even if she wanted to. Something about the way she'd listened to my garage story without telling me what I should've done instead, how I should have been stronger. But before I could get the answer out of my mouth, she went on.

"Do you trust *anybody*?"

"Well, yeah." I swallowed. "My dad. My friend Jake. And Val."

"Is Val your girlfriend?"

"Not exactly." I pulled the magazine out from under my butt and set it on the shelf next to me, which held a volleyball and a soccer ball. Above the shelf, Nicki had plastered a poster of some guy with a movie-star tan riding a surfboard, glistening in the sun and spray. Feeling a lot paler and even more out of shape than I'd felt five minutes ago, I wrenched my eyes away from that picture.

Nicki opened another bottle and began to paint her pointer finger light blue. "What do you mean? Is she or isn't she?"

Might as well say it. "No."

"Why not?" She raised her eyes from her nails to my face. "Did she turn you down, or did you never ask?" She pointed the nail brush at me in the mirror. "Wait, let me guess. You never asked."

She was starting to know me, all right.

"It was hard to find the right moment, in between electroshock and basket weaving." Not that I'd ever had electroshock *or* basket weaving. But Nicki barreled on as if I hadn't spoken.

"You should ask her," she said.

"Forget it."

"Why not? Is she already with someone? Into girls? Does she want to be a nun?"

"No."

"Well, then." She held out her hand, admiring her two colored nails.

I was beginning to regret that I'd come over here. Did I need her dissecting my nonexistent love life? How had we gotten on this topic anyway? "She lives too far away."

"Where?"

"Brookfield."

Nicki frowned. "That's only, like, three hours away."

"By car. Which I don't have."

She sighed. "You give up too easily." Her voice took on a teacherish tone, in bizarre contrast to her dirty bare feet, too-small T-shirt with cartoon rabbits on the front, and gaudy nail polish. "If you want to get anywhere in life, you have to take charge. Be persistent." She picked out a bottle of polish and shook it. "Take me—I'm looking for another psychic."

I groaned.

"No, I'm serious. I'll find a better one. I mean, I was kind of stupid to think a great psychic would be living in Seaton, the ass pimple of the country."

"Nicki—" I softened my voice as much as I could. "Why don't you give up on that?"

"Because I loved my dad. And I want to talk to him. Like I just finished telling you, I don't give up."

Well, that was simple enough. Too bad it was also impossible.

She slathered the next shade of polish on her middle fingernail, a grayish color this time. I made out the word "pewter" on the bottle, which was a good name for something so ugly.

"I'm going to take you to see Val," she announced.

"What?"

"We'll take Matt's truck. I'll drive, because I'll bet anything you can't drive a truck. All you need to do is buy the gas. And when we get there, I'll even tell you what to say to Val, if you can't handle that part, either." She waved her hand, with its wet nail, in the air.

"You can't drive."

"I'm not old enough to get a license, but I can drive. Everybody in my family learns to drive when they're, like, thirteen. I do it all the time."

"We're not going to see Val." I wanted to see her so badly that my nerves buzzed, sizzled, nearly shorted out when Nicki announced her plan. But I wasn't crazy enough to jump into Matt Thornton's wreck for an illegal six-hour round trip with a girl who would apparently have fingernails in ten different colors by then and whose main interest in life was hunting down the spirit of her late father.

"Yeah, we are."

"Why do you even care?"

"For one thing, I owe you for coming to the psychic with me. And I like driving. It's fun."

"But—"

"Besides, you need to stop secretly pining away for this girl. It's agonizing to watch."

"I'm not 'secretly pining away.'" God, I hated that. It reminded me of Amy Trillis. My face stung, and I almost threw a pillow at Nicki. "Geez, stick to running your own life."

"Don't you *want* to go?" She turned to face me. "How long can you keep wanting something and not asking for it? It's like—"

She stopped, and her words hung in the air. Maybe she was starting to guess that my whole life was about wanting and not asking. Wanting and not doing. Holding back.

TEN

A thudding woke me in the middle of the night. I turned over, willing it to stop, but it didn't. Layer after layer of sleep peeled off until finally I was staring at the ceiling. The noise was familiar but I couldn't place it, and I didn't know why I would be hearing it at—I rolled over to look at the glowing numbers on my clock—1:12 in the morning.

I climbed out of bed and followed the noise out of my room, down the hall, down the stairs. I paused in the living room, where moonlight poured in the giant windows and silvered the furniture. The noise was below me, and louder, coming from the workout room. My dad was snoring away upstairs, so I knew who must be down there. I asked myself if I really wanted to know why she was jogging in the middle of the night, and then I took the stairs down.

Mom pounded away on the treadmill, sweat shining on her skin, earbuds blocking out everything around her. She must have felt my eyes on her, because she glanced back at me and pulled one ear free. "What are you doing up at this hour?"

"I could ask you the same thing."

"I didn't get my workout in yet today. Long day."

I didn't ask why she hadn't just gone to bed, said screw the treadmill. My mother worked out on her workout days, no matter what. If it took her until 1:12 in the morning to reach that item on her to-do list, then she ran at 1:12. She didn't even break stride as she looked at me.

"Is something wrong?" she asked.

Other than my mother exercising like a maniac in the middle of the night? "No."

"Are you sure you're all right?"

"Yeah, I just got up to see what the noise was." I realized the longer I stayed down here, the more she would worry, and she'd snare me in an endless loop of *are you really okay* questions. "Good night," I said and went back upstairs.

It was chokingly hot the next morning, but I ran anyway. Heat rash speckled my arms, and I kept running. When you start training, it's too easy to find excuses not to do it. The trick is to forget about excuses and decide to run no matter what.

On the other hand, maybe you can take "no excuses" too far—since it's probably the same attitude that puts people on treadmills in the middle of the night.

I ran to the quarry and walked along its edge, kicking a few stones into the pit below. I thought about falling, flying through the air. Landing, of course, was the problem. If only I could have that drop, the wind against my skin, without the splat at the bottom. It reminded me of a T-shirt Jake used to wear sometimes: GRAVITY'S A BITCH.

I'd read books about people who flew small planes and gliders and hot-air balloons, but none of those things would give me exactly what I wanted. Maybe bungee jumping? Parachuting?

Back home, I got online and started looking up skydiving places. There were a few not too far away; they let you make tandem jumps with only one day's training.

I sent Jake a message ("You there?") because I wanted to kick around the skydiving idea, but he didn't answer. Which was strange, because Jake was always there. On the other hand, maybe it was good that he wasn't. Maybe he'd finally left his room.

I had one message from Nicki: details of our trip to Val's, which she wanted to do tomorrow. I dialed Val's number. My finger hovered over the Send button as if the way I pushed it would determine how the call went, as if I had to touch it in exactly the right way.

"Really? You're going to be here tomorrow?" Val said.

"Yeah, a friend of mine is driving there. Visiting her cousin." That was the cover story. I couldn't tell Val we were coming all the way to Brookfield to see her. Not until I knew whether she wanted to see me.

"Well, you have to come by. Will you have time?"

"We can manage it." Yeah, we could probably find time for the whole purpose of our trip. "We should be there around eleven."

"You can have lunch here. That's great; I can't wait to see you."

Can't wait. Was she just being nice? Thinking it would be fun to see an old friend? Or was there another thread in her voice?

Maybe I should just be glad that she wanted to see me. Maybe I should get the hell off the phone before I said too much.

"See you tomorrow," I said. My stomach rolled over, and it felt like a hummingbird was stuck in my throat. Tomorrow. After all this time, after four long months, I would be with Val tomorrow.

"A girl was here to see you this morning, while you were out running," Mom said to me at dinner that night. "I've seen her in the neighborhood before—I can't remember her name—"

"Girl?" I said. It took me a minute to realize who she meant. "Oh, Nicki Thornton. She lives down on Route 7." I picked a sliver of onion out of my green beans. "That reminds me, we're doing a hike tomorrow, bringing a lunch and everything." That would explain my being out of the house all day.

"Make sure you bring your phone so I can reach you. Is she your girlfriend?"

"No."

"She would be a very pretty girl if she'd had braces," my mother said. "Those teeth!"

"There's nothing wrong with her teeth."

"She has an overbite." Mom stuck her teeth out at my father. "Like this."

"She doesn't look like that." Maybe Nicki had a little overbite; I'd never really noticed. My mother had gone gargoyle with her imitation.

"Thank God you never needed braces. Although, I don't know, your bottom teeth are slightly uneven. It doesn't show much, but sometimes I think we should have done that little extra bit—"

"Ryan doesn't need braces," Dad cut in.

"No, he doesn't *need* them, but it would be an enhancement."

"I don't need to be enhanced, thanks," I said.

We all went back to chewing. The thought of seeing Val tomorrow made me want to fly right out of my chair. It was the same feeling I'd had at the edge of the quarry—how I wanted to jump, to fall without landing.

"You're awfully quiet tonight," my mother said to me after a long pause.

Before Dr. Briggs went on vacation, we'd had a family session where my mother complained that I never told my parents anything, and they wanted to know what was going on with me. So I said, "I was thinking about skydiving. I'd like to try it."

Their forks froze. Their mouths paused in midchew. I wasn't sure, but they might've stopped breathing, too.

"I know it's expensive. But I was looking it up online today, and it only costs two hundred bucks for a one-day session. Less per person if you can get a group." Not that I had any idea who would want to join a skydiving group with me. "Maybe I could do it for my birthday. They're open all year."

"No," my father said.

"Are you out of your mind?" My mother's fork clattered to the table. "You think we're going to let you jump out of a *plane*?"

"Absolutely not," Dad said. His face was gray and rigid. Concrete.

"Don't they have an age requirement?" Mom asked.

I hadn't checked. But now that she brought it up, it wouldn't surprise me if they did.

"There's no way I would allow that. What kind of parents would let their children jump out of airplanes? It's insane." Mom's face went pink on the last word.

"Where did you get this idea?" Dad asked, frozen lipped.

"I was—" I stopped before I could mention the quarry. The way they were acting right now, I was sure they would forbid me to go there if they knew. "I was thinking it would be fun." It was the truth, but I choked on the word "fun" because they looked so horrified. "Mom was asking what I wanted, a couple of weeks ago. She said I never tell you guys what I want."

They ate in silence, my mother chopping her green beans into equal segments, my father still looking like he'd taken a shot of novocaine to the jaw. Okay, so much for telling my parents what was going on with me.

"Have you talked to Dr. Briggs about this?" Dad asked.

"She's on vacation this month."

"There's no need to discuss it," Mom said. "Ryan is not doing this. No place would let a boy that age jump without parental permission, and we're certainly not giving it. *Right?*"

"Why are you looking at me that way?" Dad asked her.

"Because you're the one always pushing him to do more, to be independent. Trust him, you keep telling me. Let him have a life. And this is the kind of nonsense he comes up with." She breathed in sharply, then groped for her water glass.

My father set down his knife and fork. "Ryan."

"Yeah?"

"Are you sure you're not thinking about—" Apparently he was waiting for me to finish that sentence, to know where he was going. When I didn't, he burst out, "You just said you want to jump out of a plane. Do you really plan to pull the cord on the way down?"

I coughed, spraying squash and beans. "What?"

He pushed my milk glass toward me. "You heard me."

I drank and cleared my throat. My mother's eyes were gigantic, her face a soapy color. I wished I had never brought this up. "Of course I'm going to pull the cord. Most places you do a tandem jump anyway, and the instructor pulls the cord. It's not even a question."

"Because I don't see why you would want to do something so dangerous," he went on.

"God. I just thought it would be fun. I don't even think it's that dangerous. You hardly ever hear about accidents—not like with driving a car, and you drive all the time."

Maybe I shouldn't have said that about cars. Maybe it reminded him of the garage. He took a long slow sip of water. "Well, the answer is no."

"Yeah, I'm getting that."

We went back to eating, the only sounds the scrape and ring of silverware against plates.

I did intend to pull the cord. I had never thought of doing anything else, because to me skydiving was about living, not about death and depression. And though it amazed me that my father

thought I wouldn't pull the cord, it probably shouldn't have.

People were looking for that in me now. Maybe they always would. If they knew about me, they would watch for signs, and would see them even when they weren't there.

I sent a message to Jake as soon as I got upstairs: a video clip of someone throwing rutabagas out of a helicopter.

"What's up?" he wrote back.

"Not much." I almost told him about seeing Val tomorrow, but I didn't want him to feel left out. If I'd known he and Val were getting together without me, it would've stuck in my throat. "You?"

"Shit nothing. My Amazing Brother won a freakin trophy at freakin soccer camp. Like the 457th trophy of his lifetime."

Jake's brother was also known as the Magnificent One, the Perfect Son, and the Kid Who Could Do Anything. "Well he can't fly can he?"

"Maybe. He just hasn't TRIED yet."

"Btw, do you think it's crazy to want to jump out of a plane?"

"Yup."

"I mean, with a parachute."

"Still crazy."

"Don't you think it would be fun?"

"Are you saying you want to jump out of a plane?"

"Yeah, but my folks won't let me."

"Big surprise. Sounds like you need psychiatric help. Maybe a stay at Patterson Hospital . . ."

"Very funny."

"Personally I think: if you want to jump out of a plane, you should jump out of a plane, though I can't figure out why the hell you'd want to."

We sent some more messages back and forth. Usually when I disconnected from Val or Jake, I had a minute of extra emptiness, where I felt more alone than usual. But tonight that didn't hit me at all, because of the trip to Brookfield. Tonight I had Val to look forward to.

ELEVEN

Nicki looked younger than ever, sitting behind the wheel of her brother's truck. "This is never going to work," I said.

"Sure it will." She stuck a long-billed cap on her head, like a baseball cap but with COOZ'S FARM SUPPLY embroidered on it. It was true that when she had the hat on, it was harder to see how young she was. "I do this all the time. I never get stopped."

I showed her the directions I'd downloaded, but she waved them away. "Read them to me as we go. I can't read and drive."

She started the engine and shifted into reverse. "I can't believe your brother lets you take his truck," I said.

"Yeah, well, if he wants me to keep my mouth shut about the plants he's growing out back and the girls he sneaks into his room, he knows he better not complain. Though he says if I ever get caught, he'll swear I stole the keys."

"Oh, great." I had a vision of my parents picking me up at the police station. That's all they would need to send them over the edge.

"Relax, Ryan. Did anyone ever tell you you're very tense?"

I laughed. "It's come up once or twice."

"Yeah, I bet."

We stopped at a doughnut shop before we'd even gotten onto the highway, because Nicki said she needed "something to keep her going." That something turned out to be a tall coffee into which she poured a splash of milk and enough sugar to make my teeth tingle just watching. She also got a chocolate-iced doughnut with raspberry filling.

"You can't find these chocolate-raspberry ones just any-where," she said through a giant mouthful as we climbed back into the truck. "That's why I come here whenever I can."

"Uh-huh." I sipped my water. I'd decided against coffee, since Nicki thought I was already too tense.

"Seriously. You want a bite?"

"No thanks."

"Oh, you have to try it. Come on, live a little." She kept shoving the doughnut, oozing ruby jam, in my face until I took a bite just to shut her up.

"See? Isn't that good?"

The fudgy icing stuck to the roof of my mouth. The raspberry was tarter than I'd expected, not sickening-sweet. "Yes."

She laughed. "Don't sound so surprised. I wouldn't poison you."

I licked chocolate off my lips and washed it down with water. We zoomed down the entrance ramp to the highway. Nicki glided into the stream of cars like a pro. Better, in fact, than my mother, whose steering tended to be a little jerky.

"Why do you keep ruffling your hair?" Nicki asked. "Are you nervous?"

"Of course I'm nervous." I pointed out the window to distract her. "Did you see that hawk?"

"What hawk?"

"On top of that light pole. They sit up there, along the highways, and wait for roadkill."

"No, I'm too busy making sure I don't drive into the car in front of us."

Seeing the hawk made me think of flying, reminded me of skydiving. I told Nicki about it.

"That's a great idea!" she said.

"My parents don't think so." My father was obviously still upset about the whole thing. This morning he had watched me take my antidepressant, which he hadn't done in weeks. Usually my mother was the one who watched, and even she had gotten almost casual about it. But this morning, Dad had said, "Let me see it," had made me show him the pill on my tongue, had checked my mouth after I swallowed.

"Yeah, my mom would probably hate the idea, too." Nicki sighed. "She even got a little weird when I sprained my ankle playing volleyball."

My dad had never made a big deal when I got hurt playing sports—I think he was even kind of proud when I came home a little roughed up. Not that he wanted me to get seriously injured or anything, but the occasional jammed finger or twisted knee used to get me nothing more than a sympathetic backslap. But that was before the night in the garage.

"You played baseball, right?" Nicki asked.

"Yeah."

"What position?"

"Second base, usually. I was the backup shortstop and played there a few times."

"You must've been a good fielder. Could you bat at all?"

"There were guys on the team who were better than I was. I was good at running the bases, though. They usually put me at the top of the lineup."

"If you were that good, why'd you stop?"

I stared out the window. "I told you, mono."

"But you don't still have it, do you? You can play next year if you want."

"I only ever played at West Seaton. I don't know how I would stack up at Seaton High. I might not even make the team."

She shook her head. "If I stopped playing volleyball, I would miss it. Don't you miss baseball?"

I thought of all the games I watched with my father, the way my arm sometimes twitched when the second baseman made a throw, the way my legs tensed up when I watched a base runner. "I don't know, maybe."

"You sound like you miss it."

"Hey, if I want someone to analyze my feelings, I'll go to my shrink."

"Touch-y! Why don't you admit you miss it?"

I ignored her and rubbed at a spot on the windshield so I could see better.

"Come on, Ryan, what do you get out of acting like a robot?

Sometimes when you talk I hear all these layers in your voice, I can tell you *think* about things and you actually care about something, and then you close up and your voice goes dead."

I didn't answer her, but I was listening.

"You're a lot more interesting when you're not a robot. And this is going to be a looooong car ride if you shut down."

"Why do I have to do all the talking?" I said. "You talk for a while." Since we were on the subject of sports, I decided she could talk about volleyball. "Tell me about being a setter."

"You don't care about that."

"Yeah, I do. Go ahead."

She snorted. "You do not. Tell me one thing you know about volleyball."

"You get three hits to a side, not counting blocks."

That shut her up for a second. Then: "Everyone knows that."

"Come on." I took the last slug of my water. "Who's being touchy and shutting down now?"

She laughed. "Okay, I love being the setter because I get to play so much." She went quiet to maneuver around a driver who had slowed down to talk on his phone. "Ideally, I'm the second hit on every play. I have to know how everyone on the team likes to hit, and not only set it where they want, but at a place where they can hit to the open court." I could see how Nicki would like that, being in the middle of the action, calling the shots.

She talked on about close games they'd had, mistakes she'd made, her troubles learning the overhand serve. She talked about playing against a school whose ceiling was so low, the balls that hit it were still in play. "Those girls had such an advantage, because they played with it all the time, they knew how to play the ricochets."

"Home ceiling advantage," I said, and she laughed.

When she got tired of volleyball stories, I picked up a book I'd brought, but even though my eyes ran over the words, my brain kept seeing Val. I put the book down.

I couldn't stop thinking about this one time at Patterson, in the dayroom. My therapy sessions had been intensifying, with my counselor pushing me to talk about last winter, when I'd hoarded the painkillers. He wanted to know what had triggered me to buy each bottle—forcing me to relive every stupid, embarrassing, horrible moment that had sent me to the drugstore.

I'd told him how nobody at my new school would fucking talk to me. I'd told him how the mono had used me up and squeezed me dry. On this particular day, I'd started talking about giving up baseball, which was the only thing I'd ever been good at—good enough for people to remember my name sometimes.

My counselor had made me talk about the sense I had that if I disappeared, nobody would remember I'd even been here, because nothing about me stood out. I was one of those ordinary boring people who don't matter, who never do anything worth noticing. And that was itself a boring problem—not like the problems I heard about in Group every day. So I'd collapsed in the dayroom after my session, seething with self-loathing, feeling like I would bleed from every cell if I moved more than an inch.

Val stalked in then. I pulled myself out of my fog long enough to notice the tears in her eyes, the pinched line of her mouth. "Do you ever think this world is a totally unfair, pointless, fucked-up place?" she said, plunking herself down next to me. Val didn't often talk that way. I did, all the time, and so did Jake. When Val got bothered, she would pull on her hair or pick her nails or tap her foot, but she rarely gave in to despair.

And usually I would've said something like, "Oh, you're just finding that out?" or, "Yeah, I've noticed that a couple thousand times." But I didn't say it. I wanted to ask her what was the matter, but I didn't have it in me. A dense clot of misery filled my stomach, chest, and throat, leaving no room for anything else. Except, around its edges, the pull I had toward Val stirred.

I put out my hand, but I wasn't sure she would let me touch her just then, so I rested my hand on the edge of her chair. She looked down at my hand. Then she put her hand on my chair, and we sat like that for a minute.

Jake came in, holding the mushy soccer ball that served as one of our pieces of "recreational equipment." "I signed out the ball," he said. "You guys want to kick it around the yard?"

Val lifted her chin. "Oh, yeah," she said. "I want to kick the hell out of that ball."

Jake and I gaped, and then we broke into laughter at the same moment.

It stuck in my mind because, as terrible as that day had been, in some ways it was a great day. It wouldn't be an exaggeration to say that Val's hand on my chair was one of the things that kept me going, that made me think I could stand to keep living.

Nicki drove well, never speeding, eyes laser sharp on the road. "Time for some music," she announced, clicking on the radio. While I was answering my mother's second inane text of the day ("Do you want oranges or peaches when I go to the market?"), Nicki found a country station and sang along. Loudly. Just when I was about to overdose on cowboys and heartbreak, she turned down the music and said, "What's this girl's name again?"

"Val."

"Val." She repeated it as if tasting the name. "Does she know you like her?"

"I don't know. Maybe."

"Have you ever kissed her?"

I laughed. "No."

"Have you ever kissed anyone?"

"Yeah."

Her lips puckered as she concentrated on the road. Or maybe on the next question, which was "Have you ever had sex?"

"What? Why do you want to know that?"

"Just wondering. We've got at least another hour to kill; we might as well talk about something."

"Then why don't you tell me about *your* sex life."

She frowned. "You really want to know?"

"Yeah, why not." I rolled down the window and let the breeze hit me full force.

"Well, I had a boyfriend last year. He was a few years older than I was—my mother hated him."

"I bet she did."

"I slept with him, though I probably shouldn't have. At the time I thought he was so great and we had this tremendous love and all—and it turned out he was hooking up with his old girlfriend the whole time I was seeing him."

"Where'd you find an asshole like that?"

She rolled her eyes. "He lived next door to one of my friends."

"No, I mean, what made you go with him in the first place? You could do a lot better."

She gave an embarrassed half-laugh. "He had these amazing eyes. And he would drop his voice when he talked to me"—she demonstrated—"*like this*." She cleared her throat and went on in her regular voice. "Like he was telling secrets, and everything was just between us. Now I know it was all bullshit, but he seemed so *sincere*. And he had this great shaggy beard—"

"Beard! How old *was* this guy?"

"Eighteen," she said softly, her eyes on the road.

I knew she was fifteen now, which meant this guy must've been older than her by three or four years. "Isn't that kind of—"

"Don't say it." Her mouth twisted. "My mother and my brothers said it already. Matt almost beat the guy up. Anyway—" She flapped a hand, apparently trying for casualness, but whacked the rearview mirror. "Ouch. Anyway, it seems like a long time ago now. I was such a stupid little kid back then."

I didn't know what to say at first. I let the highway miles roll by. Then: "Did you like him because he was older, or in spite of it?"

"Um . . . because, I think. Yeah, because. The guys my age are all so gawky and stupid."

I became very aware of my left knee then, which was practically sticking into the gearshift, and my right knee bumping the glove compartment, and my elbows jutting out. But since I was about a year and a half older than she was, I didn't know if I counted as "older" or "her age." I was in no danger of growing a full beard yet, that was for sure. I checked to see if my hair was sticking up, but it was blowing all around from the open window.

"Well, he sounds like a prick to me," I said.

She laughed. "I told you he was. So—your turn. Are you a virgin or not?"

I'd been hoping she would forget about that question. "No."

"Who was the lucky girl?"

"Nobody you know."

"Are you sure?"

"She went to my old school."

"Come on, Ryan. I want details." She snapped her fingers. "Names, dates, who made the first move—"

"I don't think so."

"Come on. I told you mine!"

"I'll say this much. It was only one time, it wasn't the best night of my life, and she never talked to me again."

"Sheesh," Nicki said after a long pause, during which the tires ate up several miles of road. "What'd we do to deserve such crappy first times?"

I had no idea what Nicki might've done. But I was pretty sure I knew what I had done wrong.

It happened after the whole fiasco with Amy Trillis, right before we moved out of West Seaton to come live in the house in the woods.

Some guys from the baseball team talked me into going with them to this Christmas party. I barely knew the person whose house it was, and the guys from the team went off to play a drinking game in the kitchen a few minutes after we got there.

I roamed through the house with a giant plastic cup in my hand. At first I drank because I didn't know what else to do, because it kept my hands and mouth busy. And then I drank because it made everything fuzzy, out of focus, less real. It wasn't that I was happier, but I no longer gave a damn about whether I was happy or not. Finally I propped myself against a wall, and drank, and watched everyone else through my haze.

"Hiii," this girl named Serena said, grinning at me, her face shiny with the heat of the room. She was in my math class, but I'd never talked much to her. I was a little vague on her last name— Hunter? Huntington?

"Hi," I said.

"If you move, will that wall fall down?" She giggled and rubbed my shoulder.

"Where should I move to?"

"Upstairs?" She turned her head to glance at Bret Jackson, her on-again, off-again boyfriend. He was hanging all over a girl from my English class who I'd always sort of liked myself.

Serena's fingers slithered down the front of my shirt. I knew what game she was playing, but between my depression and the drinks I'd had, I didn't care. I gulped what was left in my plastic cup and dropped it on the floor. I touched Serena's arm, tentatively, expecting that would call her bluff. But she tossed her head and snuggled closer. And then her mouth was on mine, wet and beer flavored, her tongue thrust into my mouth. I kissed her back, not because it felt good but because I was hoping to get to the point where it did feel good. I was hoping it was just the shock of her sudden attack that made kissing her seem like making out with an old sponge used to mop beer off the floor. She threw another look at Bret and tugged on my shirt. "Come on, let's go upstairs."

When we were alone in an empty bedroom, with no Bret to impress, I expected her to stop, but she didn't. She lay on the striped spread of a narrow twin bed and pulled me down on top of her. My body responded to the contact, but my mind seemed to hover somewhere around the ceiling. Her breath scorched my ear. "Do you have anything?" she murmured, unzipping my pants.

"No."

She grunted and squirmed to reach into her own pocket. "It's okay; I do."

I couldn't believe she was still playing the game, forging ahead. I couldn't believe I was following her down this road, either. I knew I didn't like her much.

I didn't dislike her, either. She was nothing. But then, I was nothing, too. Nothing I did mattered. I could have sex with her or not have sex with her; it didn't matter either way.

Except maybe if I did, my numbness would break. Something would change. Losing your virginity is a big change, right? It should feel like *something*. It should be different, carry you across the bridge to some other place. Anywhere else.

I fumbled with Serena's clothes, and I fumbled with her. I struggled with the condom. I didn't have to tell her it was my first time; it was pathetically obvious. When she finally helped me into place, she turned her face away. All I could see was her clenched jaw and the strands of hair that fell across her ear. I closed my eyes and got the whole thing over with as fast as I could.

When it was done and I was trying to figure out what to do with the condom (Throw it in the wastebasket? Would whoever owned this room care?), she groaned, "Oh, God," and puked beer over the side of the bed. Then she stumbled over to the wastebasket and started gagging and puking in there. I dropped the condom into the basket and touched her back. "Are you okay?"

She kept retching. I hadn't known she was drunk, hadn't let that fact seep into my own drunken fog. My legs started to shake, partly with guilt and partly with the queasiness of watching all that puking. I found my clothes and put them on, getting my pants backward before I finally figured out the right way. I sat on the bed, staring at my hands and listening to her puke, for I don't know how long. When she stopped heaving, I brought her her clothes, but she slapped me away.

"Leave me alone," she moaned.

"I don't think I should."

"Where's Bret?"

"I don't know. Downstairs, I guess."

She began sobbing, makeup running down her face. I wanted to go home. I wanted to get into my own bed and pull up the covers and stay there for a hundred years. I wanted to rewind the last however-many-hours I had been in this room. If this was what it felt like not to be a virgin anymore, well—all I could say was, it didn't live up to the hype.

I found a friend of hers who was sober because she was driving. She sighed and went to babysit Serena, and I headed down the stairs. I hesitated on the landing when I saw Bret at the foot of the stairs, with a few of his buddies. They didn't see me.

"Did you see Serena go off with that guy?" one of them was saying.

"What guy?" Bret growled.

"That—what's his name. He's on the baseball team. That Taylor kid?"

My name is Turner.

Bret laughed. "So what?" he said, and it wasn't an *I don't give a damn about Serena* laugh, it was a *who cares about the "Taylor" kid* laugh. It was a laugh that meant nothing I did could possibly threaten or worry him. I didn't exist to him.

Would his laugh hold up if I came down the stairs in front of him, right now, with Serena's makeup smeared all over my face and shirt, with her perfume rubbed off on me, and the smell of her on my skin? Or would he just look through me? I never got to find out, because his group moved into the living room.

I escaped down the stairs and out into the night, gulping cold air, looking up at the winter stars that seemed forever far away. I was running out of options. The pane of glass had been with me for weeks now, the longest time ever. If drinking didn't make anything better, and sex didn't help, then what would?

I knew we were moving to Seaton in a couple of weeks, and I would never have to see Amy Trillis or Serena again. Surely things would get better when we moved, I told myself. We'd be living in my mother's dream house, and I'd get to start all over at a new school, and things would get better. They *had* to.

Except they hadn't.

■ ■ ■ ■ ■

As Nicki and I got closer to Brookfield, my nerves began to vibrate, shooting out random pulses that made me want to jump out of the truck. I told myself Val had already seen me at my worst. This time I would not be mute or hiding under my bed or crumpled on the floor. I was no longer living in a hospital. Whatever happened now, at least I would be starting a few notches ahead of where she'd seen me last.

She was my friend, no matter what else did or didn't happen. She wasn't Amy Trillis. But my hands shook, and I pressed them against the thighs of my jeans so Nicki wouldn't notice.

As much as I wanted to see Val, I wasn't ready when we pulled up in front of her house. I needed more time, I thought—but time for what? Was I ever going to be ready?

"Wow," Nicki said as the truck wheezed to a halt. "Her house is even bigger than yours."

It was true, but the main thing I noticed was that the Ishiharas had trimmed their bushes into corkscrew shapes. I had no doubt my mother would do the same thing if we had hedges around our house.

Val's mother, whom I'd met a couple of times at Patterson, let us in. "Come in, come in," she said, beaming at me. "Val's finishing her practicing. How are you, Ryan?"

"Good," I answered, thinking how much more loaded that question was when people knew you'd been in a place like Patterson. But what I liked most about her was that she never seemed to be waiting for me to break apart in front of her. She never tiptoed around me, the way Jake's mom did sometimes. "This is my friend Nicki. Nicki, this is Dr. Ishihara."

"So nice to meet you." Dr. Ishihara shook Nicki's hand as if she'd been waiting all her life to meet her. Yes, Val's mom was practically the nicest person I'd ever met. Another case of blame-the-parents-for-the-psycho-kid not exactly working. Not that she was perfect. From listening to Val in Group, I knew the kind of pressure she put on Val to be good at everything—not just good: superior. Whether she meant to or not, she leaned on Val.

Dr. Ishihara gave us lemonade and dragged random facts about school from us. My phone buzzed in my pocket and I pulled it out, jabbed at the keys, and sent a one-word lie in response to my mom's latest text ("It looks like rain. Do you have your raincoat?"). Nicki swung her legs under the kitchen table and studied the paint-ings on the wall, abstracts painted by Val: cubes and angles in one picture, green swirls in another—swirls that reminded me of the painting in my own room. All the while, I listened to Val's playing. It was the violin just now, something dark and complicated that sounded as if the strings were living nerves, part of Val's body. It was all I could do to stay at that table, making polite small talk with her mother, instead of tearing upstairs and throwing myself at her.

The music stopped, and a couple of minutes later Val bounded down the steps.

"Why didn't you tell me Ryan was here?" she said, running into the room, her eyes on me. Finally, Val.

TWELVE

Val made us sandwiches, and we sat around the kitchen table. We talked about Nicki's imaginary cousin, our excuse for being in Brookfield in the first place. We talked about how Nicki looked young to have a driver's license ("I get that all the time," Nicki said, in a bored drawl that made her suddenly sound thirty). We talked about Val's haircut. She turned to show us the back, where the triangular piece was cut out.

"That's so cool," Nicki said, biting a potato chip. "I wish my hair was straight so I could do that."

Val sat across from me, and I watched every bite of food she took, though I tried not to—flashing back to Amy, and what she'd said about "the creepy guy who's always staring at me." But unlike Amy, Val watched me, too. Her whole face seemed to hold back a smile, as if she didn't want her mom and Nicki to see everything she wished she could say to me.

She took small, precise nibbles of her sandwich. I tried not to slop chicken salad on the table or crunch the chips too loudly. Nicki rattled on to Val's mom, and I was grateful for every syllable that kept Dr. Ishihara's eyes anywhere but on Val and me. I had the feeling that Nicki had taken on my connecting with Val as a personal project; she was going to make this match or die trying.

Once Val's foot brushed my leg under the table. The table was so broad she had to reach, to stretch her leg out in a slow-motion kick, so I knew it wasn't an accident. Her toes touched my shin for an instant. My hand jerked, and I dropped a pickle round. A smile flashed across Val's face, and I smiled back.

Nicki noticed. She asked Val's mom about the paintings on the wall, pointing at the side of the room farthest from Val and me. I licked salt off my lips. Val dabbed mayo from the corner of her mouth.

"Well," Nicki said, after inhaling two tuna sandwiches, "I'd better go see my cousin now, if I'm gonna. I'll be back in a couple of hours."

I followed her to the front door to whisper, "Where are you going?"

"I'll just drive around. We passed a park on the way in, and a bunch of stores—I'll hang out somewhere. Be back at four." Then she crooked a finger at me, beckoning until I bent forward, until my ear was right in front of her mouth. "Tell her," she whispered. "Don't you dare chicken out." Then, grinning, she slipped out the door. I stood alone in the front hall for a minute, gathering myself to face Val again, to take the chance Nicki had driven me out here to take.

When I returned to the kitchen, I found that Dr. Ishihara had vanished, too.

"Mom said she'd let us catch up." Val stretched, lifting her arms above her head and curving her body toward me. All I wanted was to look at her. It had been so long since we'd been in the same room. And for a few minutes, that's all I could do: stand there drinking her in, without saying a word.

"It's good to see you," Val said at last. "I miss hanging with you and Jake."

"Me, too."

"How are you, really?" She picked at her place mat, pulled at loose threads.

"I'm good. You?"

She nodded and ducked her head, so that her hair bounced against her cheek in one glossy sheet. I had forgotten that she did that, ducked her head when she got self-conscious. Then she lifted her chin again.

"Have you heard from Jake lately?" Val asked.

I sat across from her. "Yeah. Almost every day."

She frowned. "I'm worried about him. He's so nervous about school starting." She twirled a strand of hair. "He has a tough time at school."

"How do you know?"

"He writes me about it all the time. Hasn't he told you? How the kids make fun of him, steal his gym shorts, dunk his head in the toilet—you know. The standard crapfest. And now he's worried it'll be worse, since they know about Patterson." She ran a fingertip along the edge of her bottom lip. I wished I could put my own fingertip there, or my mouth.

"Is it like that for you, too?" she asked, and I forced my mind back to school troubles, to Jake.

"Nah, mostly people leave me alone. Kind of like I'm carrying smallpox." But if I had to be totally honest, I avoided people as much as they avoided me. "Jake didn't tell me all that. He kind of hinted at it, but—"

"I'm not surprised he didn't tell you the worst. He looks up to you."

I choked on my last mouthful of lemonade. "Jake looks up to me? Why?"

"Oh, you know. Because you got out of the hospital before he did. But more than that—you changed at Patterson." She stared over my shoulder, as if seeing a film of my earlier self projected on the wall behind me. "When you first got there, you were always talking about how you wanted to die. And you had this—kind of a shield around you. But you broke out of that. Not all the time, but you had your moments."

I pressed the cold glass between my hands.

Her eyes refocused on me. "And you still—you look good, Ryan. You had this way of checking out—I'd be sitting with you or you'd be talking in Group, and all of a sudden it was like you turned into a statue. Your body was there, but you weren't. Now you're really here."

She'd told me that at Patterson, too. Before Val, I hadn't realized that other people could tell when I went numb. I found it hard to believe that people noticed anything about me at all. But Val always noticed, and so did Jake.

"I want to show you some messages Jake sent me." Val put our empty glasses in the sink and reached out a hand to me. I didn't know if I was supposed to take it or if she just meant it as a *follow me* gesture. So I kept my hands at my sides and followed her.

Val's room. I'd tried to imagine it, and her in it, a million times. It fit her perfectly. Pale green walls—not the hospital green of Patterson, but the color of new ferns. A wooden floor, and a wooden desk in front of the window. Posters of abstract art on the walls, bold shapes with sharp edges, snarls and tangles of black lines. One corner of the room held a music stand and her instrument cases.

So this was where Val sent messages to me. And practiced her music. And slept. And undressed.

She sat down at her computer. I stood over her, trying not to breathe on her neck, while she brought up an old message from Jake:

"Val, I can't take it anymore. I can't. At this school I was a loser & that's all I'll ever be. They all know why I left before finals last year, and now I have to repeat some classes & the whole thing's a mess. September's going to suck so bad. You're doing OK because of your music, Ryan seems to be doing OK, but I'm not. I don't know why I always have to be the loser, the one who can't get his shit together, & I'm sick of it."

I was sorry then I hadn't told Jake more about what May and June had been like for me, the way I'd moved in a people-free zone at school. Maybe he would've felt less alone if I'd told him more of the truth.

"My folks keep nagging me," Jake's message went on. "Nagging me to 'go to parties' and 'join teams.' Like, HELLO, nobody's inviting me! Do they not get that?"

"Shit," I muttered. Val clicked to scroll down, so I could read more.

"Some days I don't even get out of bed. I hate this place. I hate my life. It's worse than at Patterson cuz at least then I had you guys."

"Did you write him back?" I asked Val.

"Of course. I was worried to death. But he backtracked, said he was sorry for 'whining,' that he was just in a bad mood."

"Maybe he was."

"Do you believe that?"

"No."

"Exactly. Me, either."

We stared at the computer, at Jake's misery seared into the screen. I swallowed and the sound of it seemed to bounce off the walls, echo like a crack of thunder.

She sighed. She clicked on something, and dark piano music poured from her computer. It reminded me of the music she'd played for us when she came back to Patterson—reminded me of that night, and her hand circling my wrist.

I looked at her wrist, pictured myself reaching down and circling it that way. It was the gesture I always thought of when I thought of Val, the one time I'd felt that she might want me the way I wanted her. I didn't move, though, and she pushed back from her computer and stood up. She turned to face me. I should've stepped back to let her move away from the desk chair, but I didn't. I stared at her, itching because I wanted to touch her so badly, words piling up in my throat.

I did it. I circled her wrist with my hand.

She froze when I touched her. I didn't know if that was good or bad.

I hadn't been this close to anyone since . . . I couldn't even remember. Hadn't touched anyone, especially not a girl. It was almost like I'd forgotten that other people's skin could be warm, that a pulse beat inside them. Nicki had touched me the day I'd told her about the garage, had rested her hand on my back, but that didn't count. This was *Val.*

I waited and waited for her to respond. She didn't move away from me. She didn't lean into me.

I let my thumb move against her wrist, stroking the thin skin with the blue vessels showing through. She was so still that I wondered if she was holding her breath; by that point, I was holding mine.

I managed to look up. The fringe of lashes above her eyes barely flickered. Her irises were brown, cool, and deep. Her lip quivered and I thought she was going to say something, but instead she went still again. I wanted to move closer—and yet, I waited for a sign from her. At least she wasn't pulling away. Her arm stayed steady under my touch.

I tilted my head forward. My lips almost brushed hers.

Almost.

She pulled her face away, only an inch, but that was far enough. I dropped her wrist and stepped back.

"Ryan—"

"Forget it. I'm sorry." I realized then what a mess I was, my shirt half untucked, my hair wild. Nicki had made me comb it before we'd rung the Ishiharas' bell, but I'd ruffled it at lunch, and now I could feel it pointing six different ways.

"Ryan." Val reached out. "Don't be—I want to explain."

"You don't have to." I kept backing away; I knocked over her metal wastebasket with a clang. The last thing I wanted was to hear her explain, to have her reject me in plain, clear, rational, slow-motion agony. *Let me get the hell out of this room.* At least she wasn't laughing, or sneering at me with her friends, but in some ways this was worse than the scene with Amy Trillis.

"I do like you," she said. I willed my ears to fill with concrete, to block her voice before she could get out the hideous suffix *as a friend*, but she never said it.

Instead she went on, "I wish we didn't live so far apart."

"What?" I'd backed into the bed. I had nowhere else to go.

"It might be different if we lived near each other," she said. "One of the things I know about myself now is that I need someone close to me. You can understand that, right?"

She had a point. I wanted to be around her all the time, too. Except I would put up with the long-distance thing if that was all I could get. "We could try," I croaked, my mouth dry.

"I'm not going to do that." Her lips compressed for a moment. "I need someone here. I can't be with someone in—short bursts, you know? Remember what Dr. Coleman said about not short-changing yourself on your real needs?"

I sat on the bed and groaned. "Don't give me TherapySpeak, okay?"

She chuckled and sat beside me. "Okay."

I turned my head away from her and said under my breath, "I know what you mean, but I want to try it anyway."

A full minute passed before she said, "I—can't. Maybe I don't like you enough for that. Or maybe we are just too far apart. I don't know; I—"

Maybe I don't like you enough for that. That was what we called Patterson Honesty: the truth, stripped down of all formalities, all politeness. At Patterson we all talked to one another that way, but out in the world people weren't that honest with each other. Usually.

She ducked her head and began to pick at the skin around her fingernails. "I used to think about you all the time when we were at Patterson. Remember lying together in the grass there?"

It was more mud than grass, but I remembered. The smell of dirt, the grit under my fingernails, the thin blades of green, all reminding us the world outside Patterson still existed. The lilac bush in the corner with a scent as thick as honey. The sky overhead, the way the sun coated us with yellow heat, a heat so heavy we closed our eyes against it. Most of all I remembered her lying just inches from me, and how I tried to narrow that space each day, whittle it down to nothing.

"A couple of times, I thought about kissing you," she said. "I knew it was against the rules, but I didn't care about that. I would've done it anyway, except—"

"You should've," I said. God, I wished she had. I wished I had.

She shook her head. "You weren't ready. I'm not sure I was ready. Even then, I wasn't sure if we were so close just because of Patterson, if that's what made us need each other. I missed you like crazy when I got out, though. You were the main reason I went back to give that recital." The scrape of her nails got louder. "But we're not at Patterson anymore."

"Fine. Forget I even brought it up." I almost stood, ready to leave that house, and then I remembered I had to wait for Nicki. Shit. Why had I touched Val? Why the hell had I said anything?

"Ryan." She rested her hand on my arm, and it was totally different from that night when she'd grabbed my wrist. No spark, no urgency this time. "I want to keep what we have now. I can't get into all that intense relationship stuff with you, and then maybe have it blow up in our faces. I really care about you."

Oh, God—the *I care about you* line. The one that was supposed to be a consolation prize for *But I don't love you.* "Don't," I said. "Don't say anything."

She nodded. We always did know when to shut up. We'd done it for each other plenty of times; we'd done it for Jake.

Sitting there with her, I wanted to melt into the bedspread. Even after everything we'd just said, and the fact that she'd torn me open and made me doubt whether I really wanted to live through the drive home, I loved her enough to want to stay with her as long as I could. Her fingers on my arm were rough-skinned and strong from playing her music, and I never wanted her to move them. And I hated myself for being that pathetic.

THIRTEEN

Nicki came half an hour later, half an hour that I spent in the living room, straining to make small talk with Val and her mother. Noticing the long stretches of silence between us, Dr. Ishihara suggested that Val play something. I almost jumped on the idea so I wouldn't have to talk anymore, but I knew that hearing any music from Val right now would cut the last thin nerve holding me together. I might break apart in their living room, head rolling this way, legs shooting off into the corner, elbow jutting up at a bizarre angle. Rather than make them see that, I said, "Val was practicing when we got here. She's probably tired." And Val said, "Yes, my arms ache, and besides, Ryan doesn't need to hear the same songs all over again." After another minute of silence, I made a brilliant comment about how cloudy it was outside. They agreed with me.

When Nicki showed up, I leaped off the couch to meet her. In answer to Val's mother's questions, she said that her imaginary cousin was fine. I thanked the Ishiharas for lunch and steered Nicki back out the door, avoiding Val's eyes the whole time.

We climbed into the truck and I made it to the end of the street, out of sight of Val's house in case anyone was watching from the window, before I bent all the way forward and banged my forehead on the dash.

Nicki braked. "Ryan."

I groaned.

"I can see you had a bad time."

I had nothing to say to that.

"You did *try*, didn't you? I mean—"

"Oh, yeah, I tried. I even tried to kiss her. I got the pullback."

Nicki winced, then gulped from a cup of iced tea she'd picked up somewhere in her hours alone. "Well, then, she's stupid."

I sat up and put on the seat belt. "Just drive."

Rain hit the windshield, spatters at first, and then the air around us dissolved into sheets of water. The tires hissed on the pavement. Nicki concentrated on the road. I thought absently that the conditions looked dangerous, but I didn't much care if we skidded into the oncoming lane or hydroplaned into a ditch—at least for myself I didn't care. I wanted Nicki to be safe, though, and I loved the way she leaned forward, both hands on the wheel, staring out through the rain-slicked glass, utterly focused on what was in front of her. "You're a good driver," I said.

"I told you, all of us are. We started driving early, and none of us has ever even had a speeding ticket." She bit her lip. "I'm starting to worry about Kent, though. I mean, he's getting high a lot now. I can't believe he won't try to drive that way sooner or later." She glanced at me. "Do you think he gets high too much?"

I remembered Kent smoking in the school bathroom and at the waterfall. Sitting with glazed eyes in study hall. "He's been high practically every time I've seen him."

She sighed.

The rain eased, and now that I had broken the ice by speaking, Nicki talked. She talked about everything and nothing, her voice a soothing, never-ending flow. She told me a few stories about Kent, including how he'd tried to catch a raccoon for a pet, and I think she said he was afraid of heights. I didn't pay much attention to the words—only to the sound, the rise and fall of her voice, and I realized that was the whole point. She was babbling for background noise, babbling so I wouldn't be stuck alone in my head with Val's voice saying, *Maybe I don't like you enough for that.* Patterson Honesty. The naked truth, whether I was ready for it or not.

Mom texted me again, and I almost threw the phone out the window. Instead I typed, "Soon," in reply to her "Getting late & weather bad. When are you coming home?" I realized I would have to stand outside for a few minutes when we got back to our neighborhood, or else my mother would think it was strange that I'd been able to hike in the rain without getting wet.

Nicki and I pulled into the lot of a rest stop. It wasn't full dark yet, but the rain had turned the world deep gray, and all the lights had come on. The half-empty lot smelled of gasoline, asphalt, rain, and French-fry grease. Nicki parked near a picnic shelter, where nobody was picnicking. One guy was walking his dog there and smoking a cigarette—a dark shape with an orange star at his mouth.

We went into the rest station and used the bathrooms and bought sodas from the vending machines. I stared at the state map on the wall, my eyes sore and gritty in the fluorescent light. The glare showed every imperfection on Nicki's face: a couple of purple dots that were zits, the pale sprinkling of freckles, the gray shadows and purple lines around her eyes. But she looked beautiful at that moment, even the rabbity way her front teeth showed. My mother was right about the overbite, though she exaggerated it, and somehow on Nicki it looked good.

Nicki scratched her cheek and stood beside me, her eyes tracing routes on the map. I thought about suggesting that we drive past our exit, drive way the hell out of here, keep driving until we hit ocean.

But then what?

I had talked like this to Dr. Briggs a dozen times: fantasized about moving away from the school where everyone knew what I had done in the garage. Away from the pink bundle in my closet. Away from the dreams of Val that were like a blister rising under my skin, swelling, wanting to burst. Dr. Briggs always said that if I left one place I would have to arrive at another, and the pain would follow me wherever I went. "Is it better to stay and face it, then, after all?" she'd asked me, in that way she had of turning statements into questions.

Nicki drank from her soda can. "Ready?" she said.

We walked out to the truck, but I didn't want to get in. "Let's sit here for a while," I said, settling on top of one of the picnic tables. I could've used the waterfall, but right now all we had was the rest stop in the rain.

She sat on the damp wood, next to me. Our sodas fizzed and crackled in the cans. Cars rumbled in and out of the lot. The dog walker had gone. It was so quiet I could hear Nicki swallow.

"Are you okay?" she asked finally.

It was what people used to ask one another at Patterson, except when we asked there, we meant it. It wasn't that surface question, expecting an automatic yes, that it is everywhere else. I took a chance that she really wanted to know and told her the truth. "No."

"Do you want to talk about it?"

"No."

She rested her hand on mine. Her skin was moist and cool from the soda can, but after a minute it warmed up. Then she took back her hand to raise her can again, to take another drink.

I put my hand on her knee. She had a hole in her jeans, and the heat and smoothness of her skin shocked me. I'd expected to feel fabric, to keep that layer between us, but my hand touched her naked knee through the frayed hole.

Her eyes flickered over my face, and her mouth opened a little. She didn't freeze up the way Val had, but I had no idea what she was thinking. If I had to describe her expression, I would've chosen "surprised." Then she reached up and rested her fingertips on the side of my face.

I realized I'd expected her to pull away or turn away, like Val had, like Amy Trillis had. But her hand stayed where it was. We were connected through her fingers on my cheek, my hand on her knee. She'd closed the circuit.

I took the COOZ'S FARM SUPPLY hat off her and dropped it on the table. She watched, saying nothing, so I took a breath and leaned in.

She didn't pull back. Her head tilted toward me, and I kissed her. She opened her mouth to mine, pressed into me.

I'd never had a girl kiss me like this. I'd had a few awkward kisses at parties, and then the whole disaster with Serena, where she wasn't kissing me so much as acting for the benefit of Bret Jackson.

But Nicki wrapped her arms around me and kissed me, over and over and over. We lay on the top of the picnic table together, so that I felt all of her body against all of mine. I ran my hands down her arms and her back, where the humid air had glued her shirt to her skin. I was scared to touch her anywhere else even though she pressed her chest, hips, thighs, into me.

I kissed her neck, which was salty from the heat. I kept expecting her to shove me away, even though she sighed and murmured in my ear. Whenever I came back to her mouth she opened hers and let me taste the cola on her tongue, again and again. I rolled on top of her and she took my weight; she never stopped kissing me back. I hadn't thought of kissing Nicki before, but now kissing her just seemed to be one of many things I hadn't even known I'd wanted.

A car drove up and parked next to our truck, its headlights glaring into the picnic shelter. The lights weren't directly on us, but a dim yellow shine washed over us, and it felt like someone had ripped my skin off. Of all the empty spaces in the lot, the driver had to choose *that* spot? I lifted my head, annoyed, and Nicki panted for breath beneath me.

In that moment, I wanted to protect her, to tell her she shouldn't be making out at a highway rest stop with an ex–mental patient who was in love with someone else. I also wanted to dip my head back down and keep kissing her. Torn exactly in half, I stayed where I was, until she said, "What is it? Are they cops or something?"

Her voice snapped me out of it. "Nicki," I said, sitting up all the way. "I'm sorry."

"Sorry about what?" She sat up, too, her hair wild around her face. I swept a tangle of it back, tried to smooth it for her. I replayed the last few minutes in my head. Why had I kissed Nicki? Why had she kissed me back? What the hell was I doing? Was there a person on earth as clueless about girls as I was?

She scooped up her hat, crushed now, and set it back on her head. "This place has no ambience," she announced. She grabbed her soda and led me back to the truck.

"Ambience," I repeated. Her attitude, the arch of her back as she jammed the cap back over her hair, and the word she'd used, shot through my confused fog the way a single shaft of light sometimes punches through a cloud, and I laughed.

FOURTEEN

Nicki hummed as she put the truck in gear. I had no idea what she was thinking. I had no idea what *I* was thinking, because my legs still wobbled and the heat under my skin hadn't ebbed yet. I wiped my mouth, sliding my eyes sideways to watch her.

"Well," she said, slurping more of her soda, "I didn't expect that to happen."

"Me, either." My mouth had gone dry, and I wanted a drink myself. I'd left my half-full can on the picnic table. But I couldn't reach out and ask for hers. Something about drinking from the same can, putting my mouth where hers had been, would make it seem like I was continuing what we'd started. Whatever that was.

She held out her soda. "Want some?"

I flinched.

"What?"

"Nothing. It was like you just read my mind." I took the can with the tips of my fingers, as if the metal might singe me.

She laughed. "I thought you didn't believe in mind reading."

"Ha ha." I drank the soda, stopping myself from gulping the whole rest of the can.

"Anyway, believe me, I definitely cannot read your mind right now."

"I wish you could," I said. "You could let me know what the hell's going on in there." I rubbed my scalp and watched the stream of headlights in the oncoming lanes, concentrated on them so I wouldn't have to listen to my own thoughts.

"Ryan, I don't even know what's going on in *my* mind. I'm— confused."

"Hey, I spend my whole life confused." I tugged at the seat belt and readjusted my legs, trying not to whack my knees against the glove compartment.

Another long pause, headlights reflecting off the shiny wet road. I calculated the distance between Nicki and me—then recalculated it, again and again. One foot? Two? Sometimes it felt closer, and my breathing sped up. Sometimes it felt like miles from the steering wheel to where I sat.

"Well," she said finally, "sometimes it's okay to be confused."

"I hope so," I said. "It's one of the few things I'm good at."

She tapped the steering wheel. "Don't laugh at this, but—I got this book out of the library one time, about this Buddhist teacher, and he kept telling his students it's okay not to know. I guess he meant that you don't have to force answers."

"Why would I laugh at that?"

"I don't know, Kent always makes fun of me if he sees me

reading or thinking about stuff like that. Like he thinks I'm too stupid."

"You're not stupid." I watched the wipers clear speckles from the windshield.

Nicki let a few more miles of road slide by, rain hissing under the tires, wipers smoothing rain off the glass in front of us, before she clicked on the radio. She hummed along, although she didn't sing the way she had this morning.

I handed back her soda. "Thanks," I said.

I had started to feel almost okay again, but the whole mess with Val lurked underneath everything. When I thought of her, my stomach dropped down a pit, so I stopped thinking of her. I rolled down the window in spite of the rain and let the breeze from the open window stream over me, let it blow all the thoughts out of my head.

Nicki dropped me off at the end of my street, so that I could let some rain fall on me to support my cover story, and so Mom wouldn't ask awkward questions about whose truck I'd gotten out of. "See ya," Nicki said, as if the rest stop hadn't happened, and I said, "Uh, yeah, thanks for the ride," whacking my arm against the door and tripping over my shoelaces in the dark.

I stumbled into my house and into the kitchen to hunt up some kind of dinner. Dad had left on another trip earlier that day, and Mom was upstairs on her computer. I microwaved a dinner and ate it out of the plastic tray, standing up by the sink. Then I checked in with Mom. "You look a little pale," she said, but I passed inspection.

Finally alone in my room, I had a message from Val: "I hope you're OK. I hope you understand."

"Don't worry about it," I sent back.

I went to bed with my mind a tangle of Val and Nicki. Val pulling away, Nicki wrapping her arms around me. I dreamed of them and kept waking up thinking of them. I thought I heard the phone ring, though I wasn't sure if I'd dreamed that. At one point, my mother's thumping on the treadmill woke me, and I stuck the pillow over my head, but I couldn't sleep that way. It was too much like suffocating.

I woke up at six with my eyeballs feeling like they'd been marinating in Tabasco sauce, but I wasn't tired. All I wanted was to go to the waterfall and let it pound my head clear. I slipped out of the house. My mother wasn't even on her computer yet, that's how early it was.

The world was wet, but the rain had stopped. A heavy gray sky pressed against the tops of the trees, and everything dripped. My feet squeezed liquid from the mud of the trail. When I got to the waterfall, I realized I'd forgotten to bring a towel, but I stripped off my shirt anyway. Then someone on the bank sat up, and I jumped.

"Hey," Nicki said.

"What are you doing here so early?"

"I could ask you that." She tossed an acorn at me.

"Couldn't sleep."

"Me, either."

God, she wasn't going to talk about it, was she, what had

happened last night? She bit her lip, gazing at a point somewhere around my kneecaps, and I kicked off my shoes.

"Too cold to go in," she said as I crept up to the edge.

"No, it's not." I sweated and shivered at the same time. I plunged into the pool, slipped and skidded on the polished rocks, slipped and skidded my way over to the cascade. Nicki yelled something at me, but I couldn't hear her words over the thundering water. I went under.

I'd forgotten about all the rain we'd had over the past few days.

I hadn't looked closely at the curtain of water before stepping into it, hadn't stopped to think about why it was stronger and louder than the last time I'd been here.

It smacked me on the head and roared in my ears, beat my shoulders raw. And then it knocked my legs from under me. I clutched at rock, at water. My face was full of water and my own hair. I got clear somehow—desperate clawing mostly—and rose on my hands and knees, dripping, gasping.

Nicki splashed in and gripped my hair. When I could, I reached up and unloosed her fingers. "Just wanted to make sure you could keep your head above water," she shouted over the roar. "You okay now?"

I nodded and crawled to the bank, where I collapsed, face-down. She flopped down next to me. When my ears stopped ringing, when my brain cleared, I said, "Water's rough today."

She laughed. "No shit." Then she rested a hand on my back. "Are you really okay?"

"Yeah."

"I don't just mean is your body okay. I mean—it was a little bit crazy to go under there today."

"Well." I rolled over. "I happen to be a little bit crazy."

"I'll say." She pried a pebble out of the mud. "I'm glad you came up here, because I wanted to ask you something."

"What?"

"Can you come with me tomorrow? I'm going to see another psychic."

"Are you serious?"

"Of course. I told you I was going to find another one."

"Nicki, I don't know what you think they're going to tell you."

She rolled the pebble in her fingers. I saw a purplish spot on her neck, got a twang in my gut as I recognized what it was, flicked my eyes away from it as fast as I could. "I have to try," she said.

"It's a waste of money," I said. "Where are you getting the money, anyway?"

Long pause. Maybe I'd overstepped. We didn't talk about it, the difference in the size of our houses, the difference in our allowances. Nicki had accepted the gas money from me the day before because she had done the driving, and since it was my friend we were seeing in the first place, that was only fair. Yet I knew we weren't equal when it came to money, no matter what Nicki wanted to pretend.

"My grandmother started a bank account for each of us when we were little," she said. "Her idea was, we could use it to go to college." She snorted. "Yeah, like putting in a few hundred bucks a year is gonna buy us four years at Harvard."

"You're using your *college* money?"

"Just some of it. It's not like there's a whole lot there to begin with. I'll be lucky if that account ends up buying my textbooks. Matt's taking two classes at community college, and he can barely afford that with what he makes at his job." She shrugged. "I'll do the same thing, work and take classes when I can."

"Your dad would probably rather have you use the money for school than visit all these—"

"Shut up!" She took a sharp breath. "I told you, it's not either-or, and besides, it's none of your business."

I wiped water off my neck, where my hair had dripped. "Okay."

"I'm going to this psychic with or without you, but I wish you'd come. After all, you owe me. I took you all the way to see—" She stopped before she said Val's name.

"Yeah, I know. I'll go with you. What time?" So what if I didn't believe in psychics, if I didn't think Nicki's father could explain himself to her satisfaction even if we could somehow talk to him? I wasn't going because I believed we could talk to a ghost; I was going for Nicki. Because I had the feeling she was going to need somebody.

My mother waited for me in the kitchen. She jumped forward, coffee splashing from the mug in her hand, the instant I walked in. "Where have you been?"

"Swimming in the stream."

"At this hour? Never mind. I need to talk to you."

She must really need to talk to me, if she didn't even comment on my soggy clothes. Her hair bristled dryly around her face; I realized with a shock that she hadn't combed it. Here it was after seven, and she hadn't washed her face or even changed out of her bathrobe yet.

"What's the matter?" I said, remembering the phone ringing in the middle of the night. Was it Dad? He flew all the time—a plane crash?

"April Carson called. They had to take Jake back to Patterson." She searched my face, leaning forward, as if she expected to have to catch me.

My stomach curled up. "Is he okay?"

"That depends. Physically, he's—all right, from what I understand. But he's not okay."

I thought about how Val and I had discussed this only yesterday, read Jake's messages, said how worried we were. But then the mess between us had pushed all that to the background.

I poured myself a cup of coffee. "Can I go see him?"

Mom gripped her mug so hard that her hands looked like claws. "I don't know if I should let you."

"Why not?"

"I wish I knew what Dr. Briggs would think. Who's on call for her this month, Dr. Solomon? Maybe I should talk to him. But he doesn't know you nearly as well—"

"I don't care who you talk to. I want to see Jake."

"At least I'll be there with you . . . I just wish I knew if it's good for you to go at all." She rested her lips on the rim of her cup without drinking, then lifted her mouth again. "April said they had no idea he was having problems again. Did you know?"

"Sort of."

Her voice scaled up. "'Sort of'? What does that mean?"

"I knew he wasn't too happy about school starting." I ran a hand through my wet hair.

"Why didn't you tell me? Why didn't you tell his parents?"

"Tell you what?"

"That Jake was in trouble."

"I couldn't tell if—I mean, just not wanting to go to school doesn't necessarily mean you're in trouble."

"If he was anything but happy, you should have told us immediately! Parents need to know these things. Do you know how dangerous it is for someone who's been depressed—"

"Anything but *happy*?" I gulped black coffee. It scalded my tongue, but somehow that felt almost good. "Nobody's happy all the time. If I went running to you every time somebody wasn't happy—"

I shut up. Her eyes bulged to the point of scaring me; her witchy hair only added to the effect.

"What? What are you saying? Are you trying to tell me you aren't happy, either?"

"No, I—"

She banged her cup down on the counter. "I don't know what to do with you. You have every reason to be happy, everything to live for—"

"I know." I did know, and I was sorry. Sorrier, probably, than she would believe.

She wheezed, gripping the handle of her cup. I took another mouthful of coffee because I didn't know what else to do.

"I blame myself," she said, her voice low now, barely squeezing out of her throat. "I should've gotten you help earlier."

"How?" I said. "You didn't know."

"I should've seen there was something wrong with you. I thought you were recovering from the mono, that you were tired from that. But I should've known it was more. I should've realized."

"Stop," I said, rubbing one eye. My other hand trembled, splashing coffee on the floor. That was usually a major offense in my mother's sterile kitchen, but today she didn't even notice. "Forget about me, okay? I'm fine."

"I hope so, Ryan. We're happy that you're getting out of the house again, getting some exercise, making friends. But then something like this happens, with Jake—and I wonder if we would know if you weren't all right."

"I'm fine."

"I wonder," she repeated, as if I hadn't said anything.

"Yes, you would know," I said. "I would tell you this time."

Maybe it was true. I wasn't sure. But it was what she needed to hear, and I couldn't let her put me on suicide watch. "Can we please go see Jake?"

She swallowed. "If Dr. Briggs—"

"She would say it's okay."

I held my mother's eyes. I would stand there without blinking all day if I had to.

"All right," she said. "We'll go to Patterson."

"Thanks." And then I remembered something else. "Do you have my pill? I haven't had it yet today."

She walked out of the kitchen, off to unlock the stash of medication they kept from me, and I pressed my wet back against the refrigerator door.

I'd started seeing Dr. Briggs in May, when I got out of Patterson. She had frizzy hair and round thick glasses. She wore bright dresses shaped like long smocks. Her office was cool green and brown, with a giant fern in the corner that always seemed ready to take over the rest of the office.

She smiled at me when we met. Not a million-dollar smile like she was trying to sell me something, but a lighter version that seemed to mean, *Yes, I see you.* She sat at the desk, but she always swiveled her chair away from it and toward me. I sat in the brown chair next to her desk. Whenever I had trouble talking, when the words clotted up in my throat, she'd lean forward, as if her energy, her extra attention, could help bring up the words. And sometimes it worked.

I never cried in her office, or had one of those breakthroughs where you suddenly figure out why you are the way you are and how to stop being that way. Not that I expected a miracle in just three months, but Dr. Briggs never bought into big splashy miracle scenarios anyway.

Sometimes we had a session with my parents—those were the hardest ones. Mom tried to get Dr. Briggs to give her instructions (*How to Repair Ryan's Brain: The Complete Guide*), but Dr. Briggs wouldn't. "Some of the questions you're asking me, you could ask Ryan," she said, and Mom pulled back in her chair.

Mostly Dr. Briggs listened. Sometimes she asked me questions, and sometimes she made suggestions. I told her about the pane of glass, the garage, the painkillers. I told her a little about Amy Trillis. I didn't tell her about the pink sweater, but I'd never told anyone that.

When she was getting ready for her vacation, she told me Dr. Solomon would be on call if I needed anything. But when it came to visiting Jake at Patterson, I didn't have to call anyone. I knew I needed to see Jake, and I knew Dr. Briggs would think so, too.

I pushed away from the refrigerator, went upstairs, and put on dry clothes. My mother's bedroom door was closed. I knocked and said, "I'm ready when you are," to the door.

She poked her head out, her hair combed now, a line of lipstick crossing her mouth. "I'll be out in a minute," she said. "Your pill is on your desk."

"Okay." I started walking toward my room, turned, and said, "You want me to bring it back here and take it in front of you?"

She hesitated, gripping the edge of her bedroom door. "Nooo," she said at last, and I felt in my gut how much that cost her, how she pulled that *no* out of her by sheer force.

FIFTEEN

We didn't talk much on the drive to Patterson. Rain splattered the windows. Mom turned on the air-conditioning, and my eyes and mouth began to dry out. A cold stream of air blasted my chin and neck, but the rest of me was hot. The air smelled like mildew and stale cigarettes, although nobody had ever smoked in this car as far as I knew. I pointed the vent away from my face.

"Jake will be happy to see you," she said.

"Mm," I said. I wondered if Val would be there, although I didn't know if she'd even heard about Jake yet. I should've called her, but the thought of talking to her made my stomach roll.

The first thing that hit me about Patterson was the smell, familiar and unchanged: sweat, bleach, the staleness of closed windows and meals cooked hours ago, the stink of fear. And then I noticed the beeping and buzzing of the locks, the clank of the doors, and the bluish fluorescent glow of the hallway lights. It felt like a hundred years ago that I'd been here, and it felt like just a couple of days.

I suddenly realized my old room wasn't mine anymore; someone else lived there now. Someone else slept on the creaky thin mattress and stared at the lightning-shaped crack in the paint above the door. And though I didn't want to come back to Patterson, that thought slid a slab of ice under my skin. It didn't make sense, but then, I had stopped expecting my life to make sense.

They didn't let us see Jake. We had totally forgotten about the rule that you couldn't have visitors for the first few days.

"Well, can you tell him I came?" I asked Marybeth at the desk, while my mother fidgeted, breathing heavily and twisting her purse handle. She'd already protested the no-visitors policy, talking about how far we'd driven, but Marybeth was unimpressed.

"You could leave a note if you want," Marybeth told me.

"That's a good idea," Mom said. "There's a card shop around the corner, Ryan. Why don't we stop in there?"

We went to the store, but I had no idea what kind of card to get. Get Well Soon? Cheer Up? Sorry You're Back in the Mental Hospital? In the end, I got him a card with a farting lizard on the cover. It reminded me of the stupid stuff we e-mailed to each other. My mother bought a huge card with roses and glitter all over it. Which struck me as strange, because she didn't know Jake that well. I was hazy on how well my mother knew Jake's, but I was starting to think they'd talked a lot more than I'd realized. I was beginning to see how much I didn't know. How much went on around me but just offstage, invisible.

■ ■ ■ ■ ■

After we dropped off the cards, I sent Val a message from my phone about Jake. I found myself listening so hard for the return ring that my ears ached, so I clicked off the phone.

Mom took me to lunch at a diner, where she arranged her food in the usual patterns. I squeezed ketchup out of a greasy plastic bottle and mashed a fry into the red blob on my plate, trying to ignore her geometric exercises. Her lips never touched her fork as she ate her fruit salad. She bared her teeth for each bite.

"I'll be glad when Dr. Briggs gets back," she said.

"Why? Need help controlling your crazy son?"

I said it without thinking. It was the kind of thing I could say to Val or Jake or Nicki and they wouldn't even blink, but she winced like I'd jammed my pickle into her eye.

"Sorry," I said.

She set her fork down. "Maybe you didn't know this, Ryan, but your illness hasn't been easy on me."

"I didn't think it was easy." I rubbed crumbs off the edge of my sandwich.

"Do you have any idea what it did to your father and me to see you so sick?"

I thought of how her mouth trembled whenever she looked at me, the screaming phone fights she'd had with the insurance company about covering my treatment, the sigh she didn't seem to realize she made whenever she dropped me off at Dr. Briggs's office. I thought of my father's face when he'd caught me in the garage, and the line between his eyes whenever he inspected my mouth to make sure I swallowed my pill.

I had once overheard part of a fight, my mother screaming, "Of course I didn't know he was in the garage!" and my father saying, "I'm not blaming you—" I'd plugged music into my ears to avoid hearing the rest of that.

Now she said, "Do you know what it was like, having to leave you in that place and drive away? Trying to figure out what we'd done wrong?"

"It's not about you," I said to my plate, to my half-eaten BLT.

"What?"

"I mean, it's not your fault." I looked up, into her face. Blotches stood out on her cheeks.

"Do you know what it's like to have a son who wants to kill himself? Because I'll tell you." The words pushed out of her mouth as if they had a force of their own, as if her lips couldn't hold them back any longer. The people in the nearest booth glanced at us, but she plowed ahead, for once oblivious to who was around us, who might overhear. "It's the worst thing you can imagine. You can't concentrate on work. You can't sleep."

I squished a cold fry into a puddle of pickle juice, willing her to stop, to shut up. I wasn't ready to hear this yet. Especially not now, not on top of Jake going back into Patterson and Val pulling away from me and Dr. Briggs on vacation.

But I listened to Mom, because I knew I had it coming.

"You want to shake him and make him promise to get better. And then you hate yourself for thinking that way. You want to fix him, but you can't. And worse than that, none of the so-called experts can guarantee to fix him, either."

Salt had spilled on the tabletop. I pressed my fingers into the white grit, thinking about the word "fix," rolling it over in my mind. Ice formed on my skin.

"You cry all night and then you go see him and he won't even speak to you." Her voice splintered. "Or if he does speak, he says he wants to die. You ask him why, and he curls up in a ball."

I fought to stay with her, to keep listening because I owed her. The sound of my own breathing echoed inside my head, and the cold headed for my bones.

"You search his room and find he's hoarded enough pain medicine to kill an elephant. When you try to talk to him, he just scratches his head or his arms. The doctors tell you he's depressed. Never mind that you've done everything for him, that you used to change his diapers and clean up his vomit in the middle of the night. That you gave him everything he ever wanted. Apparently it wasn't enough. The best you could do wasn't enough."

She was gasping for breath now, or maybe she was on the verge of crying, her voice snagging in her throat. "He's depressed. Why is he depressed? The doctors can't tell you. He *won't* tell you."

I sprinkled pepper next to the salt. She brought her hand down on mine, and I jumped. Her hand was cool and moist, a film smearing from her skin to mine, and it made my neck itch. "Ryan," she said.

"I don't know why I was depressed." It wasn't just because Amy Trillis had hated me—or, worse, thought I wasn't worth hating. It wasn't just because I'd lost almost everything I ever cared about: baseball, running, my old neighborhood, my old school.

"Do you think that's what I'm asking you now? Why don't you listen to me?"

Wasn't that exactly what she was asking? If she didn't want an explanation—the same explanation Nicki wanted from her father—then I didn't know what she wanted.

She swallowed, her lips clacking dryly, and continued her story. "Then your son comes back from the hospital. You take a job where you can be home with him all the time, even though he slips away into the woods every chance he gets. You're terrified to let him out of your sight, but you do it because he needs to get out in the world and have a life. At least, that's what his father says, and you hope he's right. The problem is, you can't ever stop walking on eggshells."

I ducked my head the way Val often did, but my mother went on. And on. She said everything she must've wanted to say to me ever since that night in the garage. Her voice ground over me, pounded me, the way the waterfall pounded me when I stood under it. I counted salt and pepper grains on the table as her words hit me, no longer able to absorb their meaning, feeling them pit my skin.

Mom stopped with a gasp. She looked around the restaurant as if she'd been plunked there by aliens and had to figure out where she was. Then she turned back to me.

"Are you still with me, Ryan?"

I couldn't speak.

"Damn it. I wanted to wait until we could do this in Dr. Briggs's office." I hadn't heard my mother curse since the day they'd taken me to Patterson, but the novelty of that didn't even dent the invisible shield around me now. She nudged my water glass closer to me. "Take a drink. Are you all right?"

I stared at the glass, thinking, *Water, water,* reminding myself what it was. Wishing for the waterfall to shock me alive. Remembering that Dr. Briggs had talked about having a special session with my mother, maybe in September.

"I did this all wrong." Mom clawed a stray hair away from the side of her face. "I just wanted to tell you—that I wish we'd known what to do—that we did our best and—I wanted to say it the right way and—then all this with Jake—being back here at Patterson—"

Mom planted her elbow on the table and clamped her forehead in her hand, so I couldn't see her face. Finally she lifted her head and tried to pull napkins out of the spring-loaded silver dispenser. The holder had been overstuffed, and the napkins tore. She struggled with the shredded paper, scratching at it.

I pressed on the dispenser so she could pull a wad of napkins free, keeping my mouth shut. I'd fucked up enough as it was. I could only guess how many years I'd chopped off my mother's life already; anything I said now might bite away more.

Wiping her mouth, she blinked wearily at me. "Are you ever going to forgive me?"

"Forgive *you*?" I said, startled because that wasn't the question. That wasn't the question at all.

The check came, interrupting us, and then she went to the ladies' room. When she returned, neither of us had an appetite for answering the questions we'd asked.

While we walked back to the car, she put her arm around me for a stiff hug. I stumbled and didn't hug her back. My feet on the sidewalk were silent. Car horns beeped faintly through the layers that muffled me. I couldn't hear my mother's voice.

Mom and I avoided each other the rest of the day.

I went for a run and stood over the edge of the quarry. I leaned over the rusted remnants of the wire fence, panting, not sure the wire would hold. I willed my mind to go blank, because no matter who I thought of—Val, Jake, my parents—I hit a sharp edge that threatened to slice me.

I went to bed early, but I hadn't fallen asleep yet when my phone beeped: Val.

"Yeah," I said, lying in the dark with the phone at my ear.

"You didn't get to see Jake? Do you know how he is?"

"No. All we could do was leave him some cards."

"God, I was afraid he would do something like this. Just yesterday—"

"I know. I remember."

A long pause; I pressed the phone closer to my ear.

"How about you, Ryan? Are you okay?"

"Yes."

"Are you sure? Because I know things got kind of—awkward—between us. I don't want you to be hurt. Especially now."

I closed my eyes, because that way I could see her clearly, clearly enough to touch—

Almost.

There was that *almost* again, the one inch that separated me from her, the maddening space that kept everything I wanted just out of reach. My voice came out rough, raw. "Come on, Val, what do you think? I'm going to kill myself over you?"

"No, I—"

"Worry about Jake, not me."

"I do worry about Jake. *And* you. Worrying is what I do, remember?" Her voice had gone brittle, reminding me of the worst days I'd seen her have at Patterson, reminding me she had fragile spots, too.

"Yeah," I said, the anger fading. "I know. How are you doing?"

"I think I'm okay. Sometimes I'm scared to death and sometimes I'm so upset with Jake I want to *cram* hope into his brain, but underneath . . . I'm all right. I'm writing music; that helps."

We stayed on the phone even though we didn't say much more—the way we used to sit together on the ugly couch in the Patterson dayroom. We always drew strength from each other, and it drove me crazy that she didn't want to take that feeling as far and deep as it could go. I hated that what we had was enough for her, that she didn't have the same hunger I had to make it more. But she'd been the one to step back, to put this space between us, and I wasn't going to push her. This time I was the one who said, "I should go."

"Good night, Ryan," she said.

And the click when I turned off my phone was like a thread breaking.

▪ ▪ ▪ ▪ ▪

I awoke the next day with everything sitting in my stomach like a meal that wouldn't digest. But I got up, ignoring the heaviness in my gut.

I couldn't worry about my mother or Jake or Val or anything else right now. I would take a run and have lunch, and then I had an appointment to talk to a dead guy.

SIXTEEN

Nicki met me in her driveway wearing a suit: a jacket and matching skirt. She'd even pulled her hair up into a bun. I almost said, "You're dressed like my mother," but bit that back. Instead I said, "Why are you dressed that way?"

"I want to look older. That last psychic didn't respect me because she thought I was a kid."

I looked at the truck and down at my own jeans and T-shirt. The truck and I were definitely going to spoil the image—even if there wasn't already something off about the way Nicki looked. "But it's like—you're trying too hard. It makes you look even younger."

She glared at me, opened the truck door, and began tossing out old paper cups and food wrappers. I came around to her side and pulled the clip out of her hair.

"Hey!" She grabbed at her head, while her curls fell around her neck.

"You look better this way. Older, too, if that's what you're after."

She peered in the side mirror. "Well, maybe so." She pointed at me. "Get over on the other side and clean the trash out of there. I can't believe Matt piled so much crap in here in just two days."

We finished cleaning and got on the road. "Where are we going?" I asked as she swung the truck onto the highway.

"Somerton." She handed me a sheet of paper. "When we get to Exit 23, start reading me the directions."

Gas stations and minimarts rolled past the windows. I realized the last thing I wanted to do on an August afternoon was sit in some psychic's house trying—and failing—to raise the dead.

And then I asked myself: Why *couldn't* we do something else? The sun was out, Nicki and I had the truck, nobody knew where we were.

"It's too hot today," I said. "Why don't we go to the beach instead?" The ocean was a good two hours away, and if I'd thought about it for half a second I would've realized nothing could distract Nicki from her great psychic quest, but for a moment I actually felt a salt breeze on my face. I saw us far away from here, with nothing better to do than dig our toes in wet sand and listen to the rise and fall of the waves.

"The beach! Where'd you come up with that?"

"I don't know. I told you, it's hot."

"It's hot every day. That's why they call this time of year 'summer.'" She paused to change lanes. "I really hope this psychic knows what she's doing."

"Don't hold your breath."

"Look, Ryan, there has to be something to all this psychic stuff, right?"

"Why?"

"I mean, lots of people believe in it and have experiences with it. They can't all be wrong."

"Yeah, they can."

She sighed. "Then why are you even here?"

"Because I don't think you should do this alone."

A mile of fast-food restaurants and banks and gas stations whizzed by our windows. At last she said, "Don't you want to know what happens after we die?" When I didn't answer, she said, "What did you think was going to happen to you, anyway?"

"What?"

"When you—you know, when you tried it. What were you expecting?"

I pressed my fingers against the car window. They left sweaty prints. "To tell you the truth, I didn't think much about it."

"How could you not think about it?"

"Well—" I smelled the garage again, the gasoline and musty cement, felt the key under my hand. "I thought it would be like sleep."

"Forever?" She shook her head. "God, I hope it's more than that."

Somerton was the blandest place I'd ever seen: a suburb like the one I lived in before my mother got the yearning to build her forest retreat. It was rectangle after rectangle of identical lots, identical houses, every last one of them a split-level ranch. I told Nicki where to turn, and we pulled up in front of a yellow house where close-sheared grass burned in the sun.

"She's supposed to be very good," Nicki said, staring at the house, making no move to open her door.

"According to who? The American Academy of Psychics?"

"According to people who've used her." Nicki's back snapped to straightness. "Come on, let's go in."

The psychic, Paula, was at least six feet tall. Her face reminded me of a chainsaw carving in a tree trunk. She examined each of us as if she could x-ray our brains. Nicki paled and seemed to shrink. I figured that if Paula was psychic, at least she had the eyes for it. And then I reminded myself I didn't believe in psychics.

She had us turn off our phones (interference with the spirit world?) and brought us into an office with dark paneling and a red carpet. Nicki and I took chairs facing Paula, who sat and studied us. I scratched my chin, and her eyes followed my hand. I put my hand back in my lap, and her eyes followed that. Nicki coughed, and Paula's eyes shifted to her.

"You wish to speak with someone important to you, someone with great meaning in your life," Paula said, her voice as deep as a man's. Her wrist bones jutted as she folded her hands.

"Yes," Nicki said.

Paula's eyes fixed on hers. Nicki stared back. Was this hypnosis? Maybe that's how Paula would make Nicki believe she'd contacted her father.

"He hears you," Paula said.

"Um, what?" Nicki said.

"He hears you. The person you seek."

Nicki rubbed her feet against the red carpet. "What—what does he have to say to me?"

Their eyes never wavered from each other. I began to feel invisible, to melt into the pattern on the chair fabric. The air in this room was heavy and brown, as if it had been hanging in here for decades. It didn't smell bad, exactly—just old.

Paula sighed and spread a broad hand over her thigh. "There are many unanswered questions."

Yeah, no kidding, I thought. *That's why we're here.*

Paula swung her head over to me. My skin prickled as her eyes pinned me to the chair. "You are blocking."

"Excuse me?"

"Your negative energy is blocking the spirit." She raised her hand to illustrate. "He cannot come through."

She turned back to Nicki. "Your friend must leave. He must wait outside."

Nicki glanced at me.

I didn't want to leave her alone in this place. What did we know about Psychic Paula, anyway? But I knew how badly Nicki wanted to talk to her father. Maybe I could sit right outside the door. Like the watchdog I was supposed to be.

Nicki rubbed her mouth. Paula sat there like a monument, heavy and still.

I was about to get up when Nicki said, "No. He stays."

"He is interfering with the connection," Paula growled.

"He *is* the connection."

What?

Paula and Nicki stared at each other so long I thought their eyeballs would dry out. Paula said, "I cannot make the connection if you insist upon blocking it. I have done my best; you stand in your own way."

Nicki stood. "That's it, then."

"As you wish."

Nicki and I were at the doorway when Paula said, "You are forgetting the payment."

Nicki whirled. "For what? You didn't do the reading."

"That is not my fault. You scheduled my time, and your own decision kept you from receiving a reading. If your friend will leave, you may still receive it, but in either case, you owe me payment."

Nicki clutched the purse she'd brought with her—I couldn't get used to seeing her with a purse—as if Paula might wrestle it away, and she marched into the hall. Paula was out of her chair and had clamped her hand on my shoulder before I could take two steps.

"Let go," I said. "You'll get your money."

She released my shoulder but stood over me while I dug out the money. "I'm paying for your *time*," I said, "because I don't believe anything else you offer is worth a crap."

"I am aware of that. I pity you and your closed mind." She aimed her giant chin at the door. "Leave my house."

"Glad to." I kept my back straight as I walked outside to where Nicki waited, but a weird quivering traveled from my stomach down my legs. An aftereffect of the adrenaline jolt, I guessed. I'd never had an allegedly psychic giant grab me and demand money before.

Nicki scowled at me. "Did you pay her?"

"Forget about it."

"I didn't want you to give her money!"

"She never would've left you alone until she got her money. Anyway, she had a point. Not that her reading would've been worth anything if we had gotten it."

"I'll pay you, then."

"Forget it."

"I don't want you to—"

"Nicki, forget it. Let's say it was my fault you didn't get your reading, and now we're even."

I followed her to the truck. It wasn't until we were back on the streets of the development, with me trying to unravel the directions in reverse, that Nicki spoke again.

"I can't believe she did it."

"Did what? Turn left here."

"Tried to kick you out."

"Well, obviously she could tell I didn't believe in this whole thing. She wanted me out of there so she could try to scam you."

Nicki's mouth curled. "Why do you think I'm so dumb? You think she could con me if you weren't there?"

"*She* thought so. Did you think she was conning you, or did you believe she was really in touch with your dad?"

"I don't know." I gave her a few more directions, and then Nicki said, "But if it *was* my dad, I think he would want you there."

"Yeah, that's what you said. What did you mean?"

She focused on the road the way she'd focused on Paula's eyes. "Because—it's going to sound weird, but—it's like my dad led me to you in the first place. I've always thought you have something to tell me about him." She heaved the wheel to the right, brought us to a stop at the curb. "And if you would just tell me, I wouldn't have to go to all these psychics." She turned to me.

"Nicki, I don't know whatever it is you think I know. I don't have the answers you—"

"You do. You've been to the same place as him. It's like—if someone went to China, and I asked them what it was like, and they wouldn't tell me." She swallowed, her face pink. "I know it's probably hard for you, and you don't want to talk about it, so, fine— that's why I'm trying the psychics. But I think you're part of this for a reason. I mean, when I first talked to you at the waterfall, you could've told me to fuck off, but you didn't. You've stuck around ever since. And that's why I don't trust any psychic who tells me to send you out of the room."

She stepped on the gas, swerved back into the road. "Anyway, Paula wasn't our only shot. We have another appointment at three."

"What?"

"Yeah, I decided to set up two appointments. I wanted to check one psychic's reading against the other. So, we don't have anything from Paula—oh, well. We'll see how the second one does."

From the way she set her lips, I wondered if we'd visit every psychic in the state. If she didn't get what she wanted from this next one, where would it end? How many would she have to see before she gave up? I'd thought that after one or two, she would see how useless this was. I had stuck by her so she wouldn't be alone when she hit that particular brick wall of reality. But now I was starting to think she might still be paying out money to psychics when she was fifty, traveling the world to find "the one" who could tell her everything.

"Nicki," I said.

"Look, Ryan, if you don't want to tell me what happened with you, I totally respect that. But then you can't complain about me going to these psychics. If you won't help me, I have to find someone who will."

What if nobody can help you? I wanted to ask, but didn't.

SEVENTEEN

Nicki whipped out another page of directions, and we followed them to a twisting, rutted dirt lane outside Kirkville. Some of the yards we passed had goats or horses in them. Most had dogs. The air smelled of clover, manure, mud, and grass—scents thick enough to taste.

I wouldn't have expected a psychic to live out here. Psychics and farms weren't connected in my mind. But then, none of the psychics had been what I'd expected.

Nicki took off her suit jacket, panting. Her shirt clung to her, and I tried not to look. For most of the day, I'd been able to forget what had happened on the picnic table at the rest stop. But at some moments, I would remember, and the air almost seemed to hum between us. I had no idea if she felt it, too, or if it was all me.

I didn't plan to ask her, either. Especially while leftover feelings for Val were mucking up my brain.

Nicki pulled the truck into a muddy driveway full of holes. I braced my hands against the roof to keep from smacking my head. "Shit," she said, "I hope I don't get stuck."

The driveway squeezed through a narrow slot between trees. We stopped to roll up the windows, and branches whacked the glass as we drove by. Finally we pulled up in front of a small brown house. Its porch sagged over broken lattices. A cat with clumpy fur, dotted with bald patches, blinked at us from the bottom step.

"Well," Nicki said. "I guess we're here."

I waited for her to open her door. I always wanted her to know we didn't have to go in these places, that she could back out if she wanted. I probably shouldn't have bothered. Knowing Nicki, she was going in these houses no matter what.

She gripped my hand, wrapped her slippery fingers around mine. "It's going to be okay, right?" she said, her eyes bright. Not happy-bright; more fever-bright.

"I don't know," I said, because I found it hard to lie to her. In the next instant I wished I'd said yes, because she so obviously needed a yes, but she laughed. The fever snapped; her eyes lost that hard glaze and came to life again. She slapped my shoulder, laughing.

"I can always depend on you," she said.

I got out and went around the front of the truck, waiting, while she climbed down (not so easy with a skirt on, I noticed, catching a flash of vanilla-colored lace). I followed her up the steps, where the cat mewed and slithered around our ankles.

The woman who came to the door looked almost as young as we were. Her long blond curls fell down to her waist, and she blinked at us with big china-doll eyes. "Come in," she said in an unbelievably high, tiny, little-girl voice, the voice of a mechanical doll. The sound of it sent a chill right up the middle of my back, as if I'd been stabbed with an icicle. If she really was psychic, her powers must be centered in her voice, as Paula's had been centered in her eyes.

We stepped into a hot, airless room, so dim I had trouble seeing my feet on the floor. Celestia, the psychic, led us through the darkness to a small box of a room lit only by candles. At first I thought the room had no windows, but when my eyes adjusted I could tell that the windows had been blocked with dark towels or blankets. So far, this house came the closest to what I'd expected for communing with the dead, although I didn't see any crystal balls.

At Celestia's gesture, we sat in low chairs, across a table from her.

Nicki pulled at her sweaty shirt. I wanted to press my lips to her neck and tell her to forget all this craziness. I looked away from her neck, away from her altogether.

Celestia bent toward us. In her place, I would've been afraid to get singed by the candles, especially if I had as much hair as she did. But she thrust her head fearlessly between the flames and rested her arms on the table. "I understand you're here to contact someone specific."

"Yes," Nicki answered, while I thought about what Celestia had said. Didn't everyone come to talk to someone specific? Did anyone drive all the way out here to talk to random dead people, just any old spirit who happened to be hanging around between worlds?

I forced myself to concentrate on what was happening in front of me.

Celestia shut her eyes and began to drone, if anyone with her shrill voice could be said to drone: "O spirits, we call upon you especially the one spirit our dear friend Nicki most greatly desires to speak with. O spirits, please hear her call and direct to us in this room at this very moment that very spirit. O spirits, please clear the way and let that one come forth, O spirits—"

Nicki's eyes darted around the room, as if the spirits might materialize and answer Celestia at any moment. I struggled to breathe in the dense, humid air. Sweat wormed its way down my back. The candles seemed to make the room hotter, small as the flames were.

Celestia's head dropped. Nicki and I glanced at each other. I got ready to jump forward and smother Celestia's head if her hair caught fire.

Silence. Just the buzz of cicadas outside, a droning that made me sleepy. The blood seemed to thicken in my veins.

"I hear them," Celestia murmured.

"What?" Nicki said.

Celestia's chin came up, and she opened her eyes. "We have made contact."

"With my dad?"

"With those spirits who are willing to appear. Do you wish to hear their message?"

Nicki nodded.

Celestia glanced at me; I didn't move. She closed her eyes

again and said, "All right. We will hear the messages."

She took a breath and began that weird drone again. "Speaking on behalf of the spirits you have summoned, the invisible ones the ones who have answered your call, we give you some of the wisdom we possess and share with you what we see that pertains to you and to your life and to your future happiness. There is a bond between the two of you here before us, a bond that must not be ignored because it is not merely an earthly bond but a spirit bond as well, a bond forged for your true spiritual purposes, and you must each learn and teach and exchange the gifts of your spirit and act as spirit messengers toward each other."

"Wait," Nicki said. "Are you talking about me and Ryan? Because I didn't come here for relationship advice. I want to talk to my father."

"The answers you have been seeking are not where you think they are and do not look the way you think they should look. In fact you may have seen them and overlooked them already. Pay attention to your spirit messenger and the message he carries and do not despair if the answer is not what you thought it would be. It is time for you to know the truth."

Celestia rambled on that way for a while, but didn't say much of anything new. The gist of it seemed to be that Nicki and I had some sort of destiny together. I guessed that was why most people came to Celestia: they wanted to hear that love was right around the corner, and she told them what they wanted to hear. But I didn't know why she hadn't listened to Nicki about what Nicki wanted, which was to know something about her father. Couldn't Celestia make up something that sounded like a father message?

Finally, she opened her eyes and sighed. "It's exhausting," she said, "to act as a vehicle that way, to use my living energy to support their message, but I do it because I believe it's important work."

Nicki just gaped at her.

"Was Nicki's father in there anywhere?" I asked.

Celestia smiled. "When people pass on, they are no longer in their fully human, fully separate form. They merge to some extent with the psychic energy of others. And I can't always distinguish exactly who is there—but I believe he may have been. I felt a very urgent energy wishing to communicate with the two of you."

Nicki's lips puckered.

"I can see that you're upset," Celestia said, "but listen, truly listen, to the words I've said. The answers are all there for you. You've been fooled over and over—you've been walking right past the answers, because they don't look the way you expect them to look."

Nicki paid. Whatever else Celestia had or hadn't done, she had given a hell of a long reading. We came out into the glare of the afternoon sun, blinking, and paused on the porch while the scrawny cat inspected our feet.

Nicki opened her mouth, but shut it again. She pulled out her car keys and stepped down to the truck.

"So what do you think?" I asked as she cranked the engine. I was curious whether she would find some meaning in that stream of words, or if she would invent meaning, build something for herself from it. Which was probably the way Celestia operated to begin with.

"Shut up," Nicki said. The truck bucked as she turned us around. "If you say 'I told you so—'"

"I wasn't going to." I braced my hands against the ceiling as we jounced back down the driveway. "I really want to know what you thought all that stuff meant."

She sniffed and wiped her nose on the back of her hand. "What did *you* think it meant?"

"I don't know. It's your father, not mine."

She pressed on the gas, and the bouncing got so violent I thought my head would pop off the end of my neck. We wallowed a minute in the mud near the entrance, then shot up onto the more level surface of the dirt road. Nicki sped down the street, the tires spitting gravel.

We hadn't gone far before she pulled into the lot of a little gas station–deli place. "I need ice cream," she said. "I must've melted off two pounds in that house, and I'm roasting."

We got big ice-cream sandwiches filled with chocolate ice cream and ate them in the parking lot. They began to drip the second we unwrapped them. I was glad we couldn't talk, that we needed all our concentration to lick the fast-melting sandwiches. When we were done, I went back into the store and bought a big bottle of water. I poured some over our sticky hands, let Nicki drink from it, and drank some myself.

"I feel almost human again," Nicki said. She took another swallow of water and burst into tears.

I didn't know what to do. I'd thought she was calm now, that the crisis had passed. I stood there stupidly while she clutched the bottle and sobbed and swiped at her cheeks.

"Nicki—" I took the bottle and tried to pat her back. I was terrible at touching people, afraid to do it too softly or too harshly, afraid she would shake off my hand. My hand hovered an inch above the damp cloth of her shirt.

She snuffled, choked down her tears. "I'm all right," she said. "Let's get out of here."

"You okay to drive?"

She nodded, and we got back in the truck. But we only went a couple of miles before she pulled off the road again, this time into the parking lot of a local cemetery. The lot consisted of just a few spaces, dirt and pebbles surrounded by blond weeds, and ours was the only vehicle there. Nicki walked straight into the graveyard and lay on her back in the shade of an enormous maple. I sat next to her.

"My dad isn't buried," she said.

"Oh," I said, for lack of a better answer.

"He was cremated. We threw his ashes off the top of Mount Pembroke."

At Patterson I'd met kids who had thought a lot about what they wanted done with their bodies after they died. I hadn't cared much about what happened to mine—I only wanted to rush to the ending, where I wouldn't have to make any more decisions. Burn me or bury me; what did I care?

"If we'd buried him instead, and I could visit his grave, do you think I'd feel closer to him? I don't feel anything at Mount Pembroke."

"I don't know. Two of my grandparents are buried, but we don't go to their graves. They're kind of far away."

Nicki turned her head toward me. "Celestia said the same things about you that I said."

"What?"

"It didn't occur to me at first—but she said practically the same thing I told you when we left Paula's. That you're the connection to my father."

Sweat collected on my forehead and inside my collar. "She didn't say that."

"She said you were a spiritual messenger. Same thing, right?"

"I don't think I have any spiritual messages." I wanted to smooth her hair where stray curls stuck up above her forehead, but I was scared to touch her. I was very aware of her breasts against the white fabric of her shirt, the curve of her hips, and the way her skirt had ridden up her thighs. I tried to forget the glimpse of her underwear I'd gotten earlier. And I hated myself for noticing any of this when we were, for God's sake, in a cemetery talking about her dead father.

"You do. You just won't tell me!"

"Nicki, what do you think I can say? I already told you what happened in the garage."

"You told me *what* you did, but you didn't say *why.* I want to know why." Her eyes fixed on mine, the pupils small black holes trying to draw me in.

What could I tell her? That some of the things she was asking for, I hadn't told Dr. Briggs, or even admitted to myself yet? That sometimes I didn't understand what the hell had driven me, and other times I thought it was way too obvious?

"What do you want to know?"

"How you felt. Were you mad? Or sad? Were you sorry?"

I didn't want to tell Nicki how it had been. I was afraid of going back into that mindspace, I realized. Afraid of going back in and not coming out.

I rubbed the sweat off my forehead. I didn't see how anything I could tell her would help, but after watching her lay herself out for these psychics, I was willing to try. I was tired of seeing her come up empty every place she'd hunted for answers. I wanted to give her *something*.

Or maybe I was kidding myself; maybe I was the one who wanted something. Maybe I even needed her to know.

"Okay," I said, and I began to tell her about it.

I'd already told her about last winter, about moving and getting mono. About our fancy house that was supposed to be the perfect place to live, the house that leaked at the seams.

Now I told her about stockpiling the painkillers, and the way I used to run my hands over the sealed caps of the containers, savoring the whole collection with its multiple lethal doses.

"I heard guys like guns better than pills," Nicki said. I thought of her father, and I would bet she did, too, though neither of us said so.

"My family's never had any guns. I didn't know where to get one—and if I did get one, I wouldn't know how to use it." To get a gun, I would've had to talk to strangers, ask questions—which was becoming impossible through my ever-thickening pane of glass. I would've had to find a gun shop and maybe get a permit, for all I knew—if they'd even sell to a minor, which I also didn't know. If I got that far, I'd have to figure out what ammunition to get, and find somebody to show me how to shoot the damn thing. Just thinking about all those steps exhausted me, and I was barely getting through the day as it was. But with the medicine, all I had to do was get a bottle and plunk it on the drugstore counter and pay the cashier. No talking, no stupid questions required.

"Not that I think you *should've* gotten a gun," Nicki said. "I didn't mean it that way."

"I know. I didn't take it that way."

My voice ran dry. Nicki went to the truck. She returned barefoot, carrying the rest of the water, and I drank. The tree's shadow stretched longer.

"Ryan, I hope you know what I mean here, but I still don't know why you wanted to die."

I took another mouthful of water. Then I told her about the fiasco with Serena, the way we'd used each other, my guilt. The way I'd left her puking in the bedroom and sent her friend in to deal with her, while I took off into the night.

Nicki's face still showed questions. I pushed on—wanting, now, to finish what I'd started. Wanting to keep on, since she'd absorbed everything I'd said with sympathetic blinks and a face that asked for more, always more, every last secret, because nothing she'd heard yet was bad enough.

I told her, choking, about Amy Trillis, about the chill I got when she looked through me. About how she'd laughed at me, and I had shriveled.

I was getting closer to the pink bundle in my closet, creeping up on it now.

The sky had begun to darken above us, to glow at the horizon. I drank more water to stall, to keep from telling the next part. Nicki lay on her side, facing me, head propped up on her hand, elbow in the grass. Green juices stained her shirt and skirt.

She rested her hand on my knee. I'd gone hoarse; my throat felt like I'd tried to swallow a cheese grater. I had never talked so much at once in my life—not even to Val and Jake. Each tap of Nicki's fingers set off invisible sparks, sparks that traveled up and down my leg, swarms of electrical pulses. I put one finger on the back of her hand, and she didn't flinch.

"Why do you go to the waterfall?" she said.

She'd asked me that before, but I guessed she thought I might give her a different answer here, now. "It feels good," I said. "You can't think about anything else while you're under there." Even talking about it filled my head with its rush and roar for a few seconds. I decided to turn the question back on her. "Why do you go?"

She shifted, her clothes rustling. "I know you don't believe in this, but I feel like I'm supposed to, like I'm meant to go there."

"I think you like it," I said. I remembered the first day I'd seen her there, the way she'd marched right into that pounding spray.

"I was scared of it. Each time I went I would stand closer, and then I put my arm under, then both arms, and finally I went under. I made myself go under because I was scared."

"Are you scared when you go under it now?"

"Yes," she said. "Aren't you?"

"Well, yeah. It wouldn't be as good if I weren't." I stopped then, because I'd never realized that before—at least I'd never put it into words.

■ ■ ■ ■ ■

Mosquitoes began to whine in our ears, but we didn't leave. My sweaty shirt had dried on my back. A breeze blew over us, and I felt like I had nowhere to go for the rest of my life.

"I wonder what my father wanted," Nicki said. Her voice was quiet, without the fever she usually had when she mentioned him.

I rested my whole hand on hers. Not asking for anything more than that, just feeling her warmth, the reminder that she was alive and real and not pulling away from me.

There was never a magic moment when I knew why dying had called to me, just like there was never a magic moment when I decided I wanted to live instead. My mother had been looking for the magic reason, I knew. She wanted an explanation. Hell, she deserved one, too.

Nicki also wanted the magic reason—more for her dad than for me—but what I'd told her was all I had to give, this spewing of the worst that was inside me.

"I'm sorry," I whispered. My knee ached and burned under her hand.

"For what?"

Where would I begin?

I had one big secret left, the one about Amy Trillis and the library.

Nicki licked her thumb and rubbed at a green smear on her skirt. "This is my mother's suit," she said. "She's going to kill me."

I handed her the water, but she sighed and said, "Forget it. I'll see what I can do with soap when I get home."

We let the darkness settle on us, and my one remaining story sat in the center of my stomach. I'd never told Dr. Briggs. I'd never told anyone at Patterson. But now this secret wanted to follow the rest, up my throat and over my tongue, out my mouth. Something in me wanted to see if Nicki could stand it, if maybe she could stand to hear this, too, since she'd heard everything else.

My throat worked, but nothing came out. Nicki sat up and put her lips next to my ear. "What is it?" she whispered, and I was glad the darkness masked us.

Last year at West Seaton, before we moved, I had fifth period study hall. By Thanksgiving, I couldn't stand to be around other people, to try to talk to them. It was easier to get a pass to the library and sit at a table by myself.

Amy Trillis and her friends went to the library, too. They pulled their chairs into a circle and giggled, texted their boyfriends, and passed lip gloss around—at least, as far as I could tell, that's what they seemed to be doing. I could see and hear them from where I sat, but I never looked directly at them. After Amy had laughed at me, I didn't want her to notice me. She seemed to have forgotten about me by now. But I couldn't stop watching her and listening to her and giving a damn about what she thought. Even though I kind of hated her at the same time.

One day she and her friends got up to cluster around the windows, to look at some guys walking past. They left their jackets and book bags and notebooks and pencils and lip gloss behind, littering the chairs and the floor. Amy left a pink sweater hanging off the edge of her chair. The girls had their backs to me.

That sweater seemed to carry the motion and scent of Amy. My stomach rumbled as if I were hungry for it. For a minute, a hot buzz roared in my ears, and then the numbness took over. Nothing mattered.

I didn't plan; I didn't think. I took two steps with my backpack in one hand, scooped the sweater into my pack, zipped it up, and went behind the bookshelf nearest the door. When they returned to their chairs, Amy didn't notice at first, but when she did she stood up, bent over, searched all around.

"My sweater! Did you see it? What happened to it? No, it was pink—no, I had it right here—"

And then they started looking around, beyond their circle. "Someone took it! Can you believe someone took it? Did anyone see anything?" The librarian came over to see what all the fuss was, and they fanned out through the library, asking people if they'd seen anything. I slipped out the door. Nobody stopped me.

And here's the thing: Nobody asked me about it later. They hadn't noticed I was even there. I saw a list Amy and her friends made of people who'd been in the library when the sweater was taken; they posted it outside the office. My name wasn't on it. I'd been right in the middle of the library, obvious to anyone who might've wanted to glance up, but nobody ever glanced up when I moved, and so nobody had seen me or paid any attention to what I was doing. I was worse than behind glass now; I'd gone invisible.

■ ■ ■ ■ ■

In the graveyard, now, I talked faster, not wanting to pause, not wanting to give Nicki the chance to speak. Because if I stopped now and she didn't say anything, or said the wrong thing, I didn't think I could take it.

I may have been invisible, but the pink sweater was way too visible. It reeked of perfume, and it was the pinkest pink I'd ever seen. I already hated it by the time I got it home. It was so obviously not mine that anyone who saw it would ask where I'd gotten it. I wrapped it in the grocery bag and stowed it on the top shelf of my closet, first at our old house and then at the new house. When we moved temporarily to Seaton to get away from the leaks, I left it in my closet at the house in the woods, hoping it would magically disappear before we came back. But when I came home from Patterson, it was waiting for me. I couldn't get away from what it meant.

When I took it, I had crossed some kind of line. I had the sweater, and Amy didn't know I had the sweater. This was the kind of thing a pathetic stalker guy would do.

I was more ashamed of this than of almost anything else I'd ever done. I *was* the pathetic stalker guy.

These were the kinds of secrets I had. Not the big secrets where anyone would feel sorry for you, would understand your pain—like losing a parent or getting a serious illness. Mine were the shameful, horrible kind. The grubby little twisted secrets, the ones where people would shrink away from me if they knew how pathetic I was.

I lived in this big fancy house like my family thought it was better than everyone else's, but in reality I was a creepy guy who stole girls' clothes. Well, one girl and one piece of clothing. But still.

"What did you do with it?" Nicki said.

"I still have it. I don't know what to do with it."

She didn't move or speak. I wished she would. I wished she would push me away and get this over with. I thought of the way Amy had laughed at me, of how Val had pulled back from me.

Nicki rubbed my knee lightly, absently. Exhausted, I wanted to prop myself against the trunk of the maple, but at the same time I didn't want to move away from her hand on my knee. As long as she was willing to touch me, which surely couldn't be much longer, I wouldn't move away.

"I know it's sick," I said.

"What?"

"That I took her sweater."

"Well—sad is what I think. Like, you must have wanted something so bad, but what you ended up taking was a sweater." Her fingers fluttered, tapped my skin through my jeans. "You keep saying how numb you were, but I don't think you were numb if you could want something that bad."

She didn't seem to think the sweater thing was as horrifying as I'd always thought, and I wasn't sure which of us was right. Because whenever I looked at that sweater, I saw myself in the future, a full-blown Crazy Stalker Guy, huddled in alleys, leering at people. The guy whose eyes nobody meets on the street. The guy who talks to himself because nobody else will talk to him. The guy who hoards other people's clothing because it's the best he can do, the closest he can come to actual human contact.

"What did your doctor say about it?" she asked.

"I never told her."

"Why not? I think you should."

"Maybe I will." Before today, I couldn't imagine telling anyone. But I'd managed to tell Nicki, and here she still was, not screaming or even cringing away from me. "I wanted to get rid of it, but—"

I stopped there, because I knew that what came next sounded crazy. I hadn't wanted to throw it out because I thought my fingerprints or the DNA from my skin cells might be on it. As if anyone who saw it in the trash would instantly know that it was stolen. As if they would spend money on forensic tests that probably wouldn't even work. Obviously I was watching too many crime shows on TV. But guilt doesn't exactly make a person rational.

I hadn't wanted to mail it back to Amy anonymously for the same reason—my guilt was all over it. I was even afraid to turn it in to the school lost and found, or to drop it at school where someone else could find it.

So I hid the sweater in my closet and wished it would melt, disintegrate, unravel into nothing. I hoped someday I would open the brown bag and not even find a single pink fiber or ball of fuzz left.

"You could burn it," Nicki said.

Burn it where? Our white marble fireplace had never been used. Any whiff of smoke would set my mother on the case worse than a detective. I couldn't do it outdoors, either, in case I accidentally set the woods on fire. I could see myself trying to explain that one to my family and the fire marshal. Some choice that would be: whether I'd rather have them think I was a stalker or an arsonist. If the thought of skydiving had sent my parents into a panic, imagine what a forest fire would do.

Besides all that, even though fire might burn off fingerprints and destroy most of the sweater, I doubted it would get every last fiber. The spot where I burned it would become my new pink sweater: a place to avoid but obsess over.

"I don't think anything with fire is a great idea," I said.

"Well, there are plenty of ways to do it, if you really want to get rid of it."

"I do," I said. And God knows I'd thought that a million times before, but the difference was that now I believed I might someday manage to do it.

All confessed out, I went quiet. Nicki lay on the ground again. When I dropped my hand, it accidentally landed in her hair. She didn't object, so I didn't move it. The crickets and cicadas made waves of sound, their chirping rising and falling and rising again, each new wave beginning before the previous one had fully subsided.

"Do you think there's any afterlife at all?" Nicki asked. Her fingers spread over the grass, the grass that covered the dead beneath us. "Heaven or reincarnation or anything like that?"

"Sometimes I think there is, but I don't know if that's just because I want there to be."

"You told me you thought death would be like sleep."

I rubbed my scalp. "Yeah."

"And that's what you wanted? Just—sleep, forever? Didn't it bother you to think of the things you'd miss, the stuff you'd never get to do again?"

"Yeah, I thought about that. Maybe that's why I waited so long. But I also thought of the crap I'd never have to go through again."

"But still. *Forever?*"

"Well, I'm still here, right?"

She fell silent, and I thought I could hear the grass breathing, the dew beading on the tips of every blade.

"Can I tell you something?" Nicki said.

"Sure."

"Come down here."

I lay beside her. She snuggled against me.

"Swear you won't tell anyone?"

"Yes."

A sigh, right into my ear. She whispered, "The week before my dad died, he took me to Funworld."

"The amusement park?"

"Yeah."

I waited.

"He skipped out on his job to do it." Her body was warm against my left side; the grass was cold under my back. The heat and chill met somewhere in the middle of me, like having a fever.

"I had so much fun," she said. "It was just the two of us. When the whole family went, Matt would only go on the roller coasters, and Kent always got sick after three rides, so this was the one time I got to go on all the rides and do everything I wanted."

Strands of her hair brushed my neck, tickling my skin. But I didn't move.

"He got in trouble, though. He'd cut out of work too many times. They fired him, and he took that really, really bad." Her breath was heavy in my ear. "Everyone in my family knows he got fired and that's one reason he probably killed himself. But they don't know about that day at Funworld. He said Mom would get mad at him, and Matt and Kent would feel left out, so we didn't tell anyone."

I listened, waiting for the big secret, for whatever she needed to whisper.

"My family still doesn't know."

"Uh-huh."

"If I'd made him go to work instead—"

"It wasn't your fault." Suddenly I understood what the big secret was—just this. What she'd already told me. She had pinned her father's death on this one day at Funworld—as if there were only one thing it *could* be pinned on.

"If he hadn't taken me to Funworld, he wouldn't have gotten fired."

"You don't know that. Besides, you said he wasn't fired because of that one day. He skipped work all the time." I shifted so that I could put my arm around her.

She shook her head with frustration that I didn't understand, that I didn't get her guilt and why she was the bad guy in this story. But the fact was, I understood exactly.

I stroked her arm the way she'd stroked mine, and she turned her face toward me. I knew that if I turned my head, I wouldn't be able to keep my mouth off hers. And I didn't fully understand it, because I couldn't forget about Val, either, even if there was no chance of anything happening there.

Nicki touched my cheek and turned my head toward hers—not that she had to push hard. Our mouths met and we almost seemed to stop breathing. I drew her on top of me so I could feel her whole body against mine, and this time I let my hands go everywhere— over her shirt, her skirt, then back over her sweaty, rumpled clothes, up to the tangle of her hair. Down again, inch by inch this time, never taking my mouth away from hers.

We kept our clothes on. I was scared of what would happen if we didn't, because right then I would have taken anything and I would have given her anything. Instead I tried to take in her whole body through my hands, through my tongue, her breath in my mouth, her hands on me.

EIGHTEEN

"Where have you been?" my mother asked the instant I walked in the door. Not only had I missed our daily check-in, but she and my father had been edgier, hovering over me a little more, since the skydiving talk. Jake's return to Patterson hadn't helped. "I kept trying your phone, and you never answered!"

"Oh—I shut it off and forgot to turn it back on." I realized now I was lucky she hadn't sent out the police.

"If you can't keep it on, maybe you should stay home."

"I'm sorry."

"I need to be able to reach you. Where *were* you?"

I kicked off my shoes. "With Nicki."

"The girl with the overbite? Again?" She followed me through the living room, into the kitchen.

"Don't say it like that's the most obvious thing about her."

"I don't like you running around with her unsupervised."

"Why?" I opened the refrigerator and stood there in my bare feet, taking stock. Diet yogurt, diet lemonade, diet soda. Urgh. I pulled out a plum and rubbed my thumb across the silver frost on its skin.

"It's too easy to get in trouble," she said.

"You mean pregnant? She's not my girlfriend, Mom." She wasn't, was she? I didn't know what the hell she was, after tonight. I'd never had a real girlfriend before, but surely there was a limit on the number of times you could make out with a friend before it became—

Mom's lips wrinkled. "Not just that. There's drinking, drugs—"

"We don't drink or do drugs, either." *We just drive around in her brother's truck visiting the psychics of the state, trying to talk to her father's ghost.*

"What *do* you do?"

"Hang out, talk. Nothing much."

I bit into the plum. We locked eyes, as if she were waiting for me to confess that Nicki and I built pipe bombs or had orgies in the woods. But I had nothing to say. I gnawed the fruit down to the woody pit and tossed it in the trash while pink crept up Mom's face. I heard her words from yesterday all over again, her voice shredding in the diner. "I'm sorry," I said again. "I should've checked my phone."

She frowned and straightened the edge of the trash bag where it lapped over the outside of the can. "I talked to Jake's mother. He's doing as well as can be expected."

"What does that mean?"

She sighed. "I'm not sure I know myself."

■ ■ ■ ■ ■

I climbed up to my room and checked my messages. I had a couple from Val; I clicked on the first one.

"Thanks for letting me know you went to Patterson. I'm glad you went, even though they wouldn't let you see Jake. At least he'll know you were there.

"I can't stand thinking about it. When I heard he slashed his wrists, it put pictures in my head that I can't get rid of. I try to prepare myself for this stuff, but I never really can.

"How are you doing with it?"

When I hadn't answered that message, because I'd been out with Nicki all day, she'd sent another.

"Now I know it's silly and I shouldn't worry, but the truth is when something like this happens I worry anyway. You know how at Patterson we talked about copycats, and I'm sure you wouldn't do anything like that really, but it's not like you've never thought about it. I remember you and Jake going on about the best ways to kill yourselves, about nooses and guns and bridges and all that, when he first got to Patterson. And even though that was months ago, he's back in the hospital now, and if you could send me a message to let me know you're OK, I would appreciate it.

"And if you're not OK, I want to know that too. Even more!"

She'd signed it, "Love, Val."

I could imagine what she'd thought when I hadn't answered that message, either. I checked the time on it: 6:23. But it wasn't just to ease her fears that I hit Reply. What was this about Jake slashing his wrists? And why hadn't I known about that sooner?

"Hey, Val. I'm here. I was away from my computer all day & had my phone off. Did you say Jake slashed his wrists? Because my mother didn't tell me that."

Val must've been waiting, because her answer zipped right back to me.

"She was probably afraid to tell you. Because of your history."

I loved that. My *history*.

"But it's true," she wrote on. "He cut himself, but it didn't work."

"Good. I mean, good that it didn't work."

A pause. Then, from her: "Are you OK?"

"Yes."

"You sure? Because you can tell me if you aren't. When I said I wanted to be your friend, I meant it. Friend isn't even a strong enough word for what you are. I love you. I hope you know that."

In some ways, when she said things like that, it was harder to take than if she'd cut me off cold. Sometimes, *almost* getting what you want is worse than never coming close.

We were still friends, though. And we had Jake to worry about. "Yeah, I'm OK. Are you?"

"Yes. But I'm mad at J. And sorry for him. I want to smack him across the face and hug him at the same time."

I hadn't felt any of that yet. It always took things forever to sink in for me. By the time I absorbed anything, the rest of the world had moved on, and I was stuck thinking about things that everyone else had left behind. I settled for typing: "I can see that."

"I wish he had talked to me. He did for a while, but he shut down near the end. Even though I was right here."

"Sometimes it's too hard."

"Bullshit. Harder than killing yourself?"

That was aimed at me, too, I knew. Jake's and my death wishes had always bothered Val; she didn't understand why we were that way. She'd always wanted to fix us. The meanest thing Jake had ever said to her, once when she'd pushed him too hard, was, "Stop worrying about *me*, and see if *you* can stop picking your nails and pulling out your eyelashes for three seconds!" And she'd shot back, "At least *my* stuff isn't fatal!"

"My mom said he was OK," I wrote now. "Was she lying about that, too, or is he really OK? I mean physically. I know he's not completely OK."

"Yeah, they just stitched him up, from what I understand."

We sent a few more messages back and forth, mostly about how we hoped Jake would make it, and then I disconnected. I paced a couple of circles around my room, wanting to go downstairs and confront my mother, to ask her what the hell she had meant by hiding this information from me.

But I already knew what she meant by it—that she didn't think I could handle it, that she was afraid it would give me ideas. And I didn't want to start a talk with her that might lead to another tidal wave like the one she'd unleashed in the restaurant.

I stopped in front of my closet and twisted the knob. The bundle sat there on its shelf.

I realized that I had told Nicki about it.

I had told her the sickest things I'd ever done, and she hadn't screamed and run away. Flames hadn't come shooting out of my head. She'd even kissed me after knowing the truth.

I'd hated this sweater for months, but now was the first time it seemed possible—actually possible, not just a fantasy—to get rid of it.

NINETEEN

The next day I got up early and ran. I thought about only one thing while I was on the trail: the sweater plan. I mapped it out, pictured the ending a hundred different ways. I told myself that the scenes where police led me off in handcuffs were ridiculous. Not even Amy Trillis would call the cops in a situation like this, would she?

Unless maybe she wanted to ask for a restraining order?

My feet smacked the dirt. Gobs of mud flew, speckling my calves and my shorts. The leaves around me smelled green, bursting, swollen with rain and chlorophyll. I tried to focus on the rhythm of my feet, but pictures of Amy flashed across my mind.

I ran harder, sweating until I thought I might dissolve. Maybe I could melt away before I ever had to confront her. I could become a puddle on the path, soak into the ground, rise up through the tree roots.

But at the end of the run, though I was heaving and soaked and coated with mud, I was still here.

▪ ▪ ▪ ▪ ▪

In the shower, I willed my mind to go blank. I told myself I had pre-
pared enough; there was nothing more to imagine. Or to "visual-
ize," as they said at Patterson. I adjusted the spray until hot needles
pelted my skin, ducked my head under and scrubbed at my scalp. If
I could've stopped time then, I would have.

I rode my bike into West Seaton, where Amy's aunt owned a restaurant called the Gingerbread Café. Amy had worked there, and I
thought she still might, or at least the people there would know her. I
didn't know her home address and didn't want to hunt for it, because
I didn't need to feel more stalkerish than I already did.

"Do you know Amy Trillis?" I asked the girl behind the counter of the café, a girl with an eyebrow ring that gave her a look of
constant surprise.

"Yeah, she's here now," the girl said. "Working in the back."

"What time does she get off?"

"Two."

It was twelve thirty. The hour and a half stretched in front of
me, but I reminded myself that I'd lived this long with the sweater.
I could stand it a little longer.

I went to the library and sat in a dark corner of the historical
section with a magazine in my hands, reading words that never
sank into my brain. The building smelled of paper and dust, com-
fortable smells.

I tried not to picture the scene with Amy. I ran over my planned
speech for the millionth time, but I tried not to imagine what she

might say, and what I might say in return. I would just have to let it happen. If she laughed, if she screamed at me, if she shrank away, if she made fun of me—no, I had to stop thinking about it.

This sweater had been weighing on me for months; I couldn't believe that today was the day I would get rid of it. Unless I changed my mind. This didn't *have* to be the day. I could go home right now and never talk to Amy—

Enough.

I was finished hiding the sweater, agonizing about someone finding it. I was finished with reliving the day I'd taken it and cringing every time. After all, Nicki knew the truth, and she hadn't told me I should be locked up.

Of course, it wasn't her sweater I'd taken.

To steer my mind off this crazy circular track, I pulled out my phone. First I had to answer a text from my mother and reassure her that I was still alive. Then I thought I could break the tension of waiting by texting something stupid to Jake—until I remembered where he was. Maybe I should send a message to Val? No. She didn't have much in common with Amy otherwise, but they'd both rejected me, and I couldn't reach out to Val right now.

What about Nicki? Maybe. Except that I wanted to wait and talk to her when this was all over. I wanted to be able to tell her I'd given back the sweater.

The brown paper bag sat on the table in front of me. I couldn't imagine how it would be not to have it anymore. It would be like an amputation, except that the sweater was more of a tumor than a limb.

▪ ▪ ▪ ▪ ▪

I waited outside the Gingerbread Café at ten of two. I sat by the bike rack, trying to look natural, feeling as if my elbows and knees stuck out. People snuck looks at me, and I knew they thought I was plan-ning to steal their bikes, but I gazed past them to show I had bigger, more important matters on my mind. I took deep breaths to calm myself down, inhaling the rubbery smell of bike tires.

Twenty minutes later, Amy finally came out, checking her phone as she walked. She wore less makeup than she had last year, but she had the same dark curls I remembered. My eyes used to trace the curves of her face, shoulder, and body. But today I marched up to her without savoring the sight of her—legs quivering, wanting to run in the other direction.

"Amy? Excuse me."

She turned her head toward me, no flash of recognition in her eyes. And yet, she didn't seem surprised that I knew her name. May-be girls like her were just used to everyone knowing who they were.

"I'm Ryan Turner. I used to go to school with you," I said. "Can I talk to you a minute?"

"I guess." She glanced at her phone and clicked something.

"This won't take long."

"Okay."

The Gingerbread had a couple of outdoor picnic tables and benches. The ones in the shade were filled, but I sat on the sunniest bench, where nobody was close enough to overhear us. Amy hov-ered, not sitting. "I have something that belongs to you." I pulled the grocery bag out of my backpack, opened the top of it, and showed it to her. She peeked in.

"What's that?"

"A sweater."

She blinked. It amazed me that she didn't grab it right away—I wasn't sure she recognized it. To me it had loomed so huge, had seemed to glow with neon brightness on my shelf, even through the brown covering. I'd pictured her searching for it every day, missing it, wondering where it had gone. Only now did I see how stupid that was.

"I took it from the library at West Seaton High last year."

"Oh, yeah, I remember! It just disappeared." She reached into the bag and pulled it out. I cringed, wishing she wouldn't hold it up in broad daylight where everyone around us could see it, forgetting that to them it would be an ordinary piece of clothing. "Yes, this is it. Wow." Her eyes flicked back to me. "You said you took it? Why?"

"I don't know," I said automatically, but I had vowed to tell the truth today, so I tried again. "It was a dumb thing to do. I guess—I had a crush on you back then." Whatever I'd felt for her had dried up so long ago that I heard the flatness in my own voice. Ever since December, when I'd taken it, that sweater had been nothing but an embarrassment to me.

"Oh." She took a step back and rolled up the sweater. "I—didn't know." I could've told her she had known, she'd once guessed how much I had liked her, but she'd obviously forgotten. It didn't matter. "Why are you bringing it back now?"

"I always felt bad about taking it, and I'm sorry."

"Well." She nodded, but without meeting my eyes. Glancing off to the side, as if checking for escape routes. "Is that all?"

"Yeah."

She stuffed the sweater back in the bag, frowning. "You know what? Would you mind if—could you put this in a Goodwill box or something?"

I almost groaned. Having finally gotten the damn thing off my hands, the last thing I wanted was to take it back. But I had to see this through. I could understand why she wouldn't want it back. So I said, "All right. If that's what you want."

"Good." She dropped the bag on the bench next to me. "Thanks," she said and walked away.

I biked over to a place on Nichols Avenue where I always used to see a clothes-drop box. It was still there. I pulled down the metal door and heaved the sweater in, bag and all. And I turned for home, with my hands empty at last.

TWENTY

I'd expected that giving up the sweater would practically make me float home. And I had minutes like that, minutes where a grin stretched my face and the pedals whipped around with no effort at all, but then dread crept over me. Amy Trillis knew my secret now. Amy Trillis, of all people. I could picture her telling everyone in West Seaton. "You'll never believe the weird thing that just happened," she could say, and the whole world would know me as Pathetic Stalker Guy.

Or—I thought, as the elation returned—she might not bother to say anything. It obviously hadn't mattered that much to her. She hadn't even wanted to take back the sweater. She seemed to want to forget the whole thing.

I realized I no longer cared if Amy Trillis thought I was weird. I'd looked her in the eye and, though I'd told her the truth, she hadn't laughed at me. I didn't especially want the world to know I'd taken her sweater, but if they did find out, I would deal with it.

I stopped in Seaton for a drink, chugging down one of those

blue energy drinks in the parking lot of a minimart, with my bike leaning against me. In front of the store, five kids from my neighborhood had gathered. I knew some of their names, but I hadn't talked much to them. They were a little younger than me.

"Is that the psycho kid?" one of them said, and I knew they were talking about me, but I kept guzzling blue fluid and staring out at the horizon. I was listening now, though.

"Yeah, I think so. Isn't he the one Nicki's always with lately?"

"Uh-huh. Man, what's wrong with her?"

They laughed. Then a girl with skinny legs and long shining hair said, "Don't worry, she promised me she's not going out with him or anything. She's just being nice to the local loser."

More laughter. "Maybe so, but what for?"

I swung my leg over the bike and pedaled off, dropping my empty bottle in a green bin on my way out of the lot. The asphalt shimmered in the heat, and their laughter dissolved behind me. But the words "local loser" were branded into my brain.

Even though I'd biked all the way home and wanted to collapse on my bed, I decided to run up to the waterfall. I had a few words for Nicki.

But Nicki wasn't there. Kent was, smoking as usual.

"Hey," he said.

"Hey." I bent over for a minute, panting, wishing I were in better shape. "Where's your sister?"

"I don't know." He blew smoke into the mist and waved at a new sign on one of the trees: NO SWIMMING OR DIVING. I hated the man-made look of the sign, its starkness and sharp corners in the middle of all this lush green, but I could understand why they'd put it up.

"Look at that," Kent said. "They keep trying, but it'll get torn down in a couple of days."

"I guess they do that because of the kid who died here. Liability or something."

Kent stared at me. "Kid? What kid?"

"Bruce what's-his-name. Nicki told me. She said she was here the day it happened."

Kent barked; you couldn't call it a laugh. "It wasn't any kid. It was our dad."

"What?"

I stepped closer. With the roar of the waterfall, I couldn't hear him too well. I thought he'd said, *It was our dad.*

"Our dad died here." Kent pointed his cigarette at the top of the cascade. "Walked out there—jumped—" The cigarette traced a path in the air. "Landed down there, headfirst. Nicki wasn't even here. Just me and Matt."

I stared, a chill and then a burn running through my whole body. "Your father?"

"I thought for sure she woulda told you. You're hanging with her all the time lately."

I wiped mist from the waterfall off my face.

"They woulda thought it was an accident, but me and Matt saw him jump. Hell, he did a fuckin' dive. Besides, he left a note."

"He left a note?" After all Nicki's wailing about *Why didn't he leave a note?* Then what—why—

"Well, not much of a note. 'I can't take it anymore, I'm sorry.' Like that was supposed to tell us something we couldn't figure out ourselves." Kent took a drag on his cigarette. "I didn't watch him land, but Matt did. I shut my eyes. I heard him land, though, like *thunk*!" Kent shuddered. "Fucked me up pretty good for a while. Matt, too. Nicki was mad because Dad didn't let her come with us that day. She shoulda been glad."

"I'm sorry," I said.

"I can't believe she didn't tell you," he said. "I can't figure her out sometimes."

I went home, to my computer. I couldn't be sure that Nicki had lied; how did I know Kent was telling the truth? And so I started searching.

The articles weren't hard to find. LOCAL MAN DIES IN SWIMMING-HOLE ACCIDENT, said the very first article. But the second article called it suicide and reported the existence, though not the contents, of the note.

Philip Thornton had jumped from the top of a waterfall while his two sons watched. His wife and daughter were at home. He broke his neck and died at the scene. The township had put saw-horse barriers and signs around the waterfall. I wondered how long it had taken the barriers to disappear.

I clicked around the computer in a haze. I checked my messages. Val wanted to know if I could meet her at Patterson next weekend to visit Jake. I told her I would. The thought of Val hurt, but it was a muffled, old-feeling ache, as if she were a broken bone that had healed and now just bothered me in the rain. I could handle seeing her if Jake needed us.

I had a message from Jake's mother, thanking me for the card and telling me he wanted to see me. I wrote her back, saying Val and I would go next weekend.

I had nothing else but spam. I got off the computer and walked over to my closet. My gut lurched when I saw that the place where the bag had always been was empty. Then I remembered: it was empty for good. The meeting with Amy seemed to have happened years ago.

I lay down and pressed my face into my pillow. I tried to forget Nicki, to erase the words "just being nice to the local loser" from my brain, along with the snickers of her friends. I wanted to forget everything she'd ever told me, but I couldn't stop it anymore, her words rushing over me—what she'd said about a boy named Bruce dying at the waterfall, and about her father having a gun, and how she needed to know why he'd done it because he hadn't even written a note—God, had she ever told me the truth about anything?

If I hadn't cut myself off from everyone at school, maybe I would've known the truth sooner. Somebody would've told me about Kent and Nicki's father before now. But I'd kept myself so insulated that only the rumor of a dead guy at the waterfall had leaked through, and I didn't trust rumors. China could envy the Great Wall I'd built around myself.

Until Nicki had come over the wall—

And I'd told her everything. My stomach folded in on itself when I thought of how much I'd spilled the night before. She already knew how I felt about Val. She knew about the garage. And now I'd told her about *Amy and the sweater*.

I flopped over and glared at the ceiling. I remembered the picnic table at the rest stop. The way she'd kissed me after that terrible day at Val's, and again when I spewed out all my worst secrets in the graveyard. I could feel the warmth of her mouth, and the way she'd pressed against me.

And I could feel her whispering her secret in my ear, last night under the tree. Had the day at Funworld with her father been real? Or had she made that up, too? What the hell had she been doing—playing with me? And why hadn't she ever told me the truth about the waterfall?

I'd met pathological liars at Patterson. Of course we all lied a little, about things we couldn't stand to admit. But there were only a few who told big lies, like the ones Nicki had told me.

I rolled over again, every word she had said to me echoing in my ears.

Something built inside me, a roar like static. I began to scratch at my skin. Whenever I felt this way at Patterson, they told me to talk it out. ("Don't act it out; talk it out," they said to the kids who liked to throw chairs; and to the kids like me they said, "Don't hold it in; talk it out.") But who did I have now? Dr. Briggs was away; I'd talked to Dr. Solomon only once.

Jake was in the hospital.

I couldn't face Val with this. I couldn't tell her that less than a week after she'd pulled away from me, another girl had made a fool out of me. I couldn't lose the last scrap of pride I had with Val, the pride of not having imploded in front of her when she rejected me.

My dad was away. I couldn't talk to my mother, not after what she'd said at the diner the other day. Not unless I wanted her to die of anxiety.

I tried to take deep breaths. I jiggled my feet, scratched at my arms, pulled threads out of my bedspread. I counted into the thousands, lost my place, and started again.

Val didn't want me. Jake was in trouble. My mother would never get over that night in the garage and my stay at Patterson. The only person I'd been able to trust recently was Nicki, and now she—

I wandered into the bathroom and opened the medicine cabinet.

After I'd been caught stockpiling painkillers, my parents had cleaned out their cabinets and closets. All our cleaners were now nontoxic, and my parents bought medicines in the tiniest bottles available. They kept my antidepressants locked up and doled them out to me one pill at a time. When I came out of Patterson, my parents and I had signed a "contract" saying that I agreed not to stockpile drugs if they would agree not to search my room. We were supposed to renew the agreement every month. But we got rid of it back in July, when I told Dr. Briggs that the only time I ever wanted to hoard drugs anymore was the one moment a month when I had to sign that stupid paper.

Now I leaned over the sink, studying those miniature bottles and boxes. Then I closed the cabinet, avoiding looking at its mirrored front.

I drifted back into my bedroom. I thought about running up to the quarry, but I had a feeling I shouldn't do that. I had a strong pull to lean over the edge today.

I would've liked to smash my bedroom windows. I ran my fingertips down the glass. They left smears; my mother would have a fit if she saw. Then I pushed against the glass, testing it. I knocked against it with my knuckles, then again, harder. The glass flexed and didn't break.

I should run, I told myself. In spite of the running and biking I'd already done that day, prickly nervous energy built in my arms and legs. Dr. Briggs would probably tell me to run, except not to the quarry. Well, what she really would do was make me talk about Nicki. About the psychics and Nicki's father and the lies. The fact that Nicki had been fucking lying to me all month and I didn't know why, that she'd curled up with me the night before and told me a story that probably wasn't even true . . . the fact that she was "just being nice" to the neighborhood psycho . . .

I took a breath. A deep, slow one, like they taught us at Patterson. Like Val taught me; she said it was good for warding off panic attacks. Not that I was going to have a panic attack. Not over Nicki; no way.

Nicki.

The thought of her made something surge up inside me, and

I pictured my fist punching through the window, although I kept standing there with my knuckles against the glass. My teeth were clamped together. I tried to relax my jaw, and my arm, which had gone rigid.

I had to get the hell out of here. I would go running, I decided.

TWENTY-ONE

I ran out the front door. At the edge of our yard, where the trail plunged into forest shade, I smacked into Nicki.

She'd been charging up the path to my house, hair flying. We bounced off each other.

"Kent said he—told you some things," she gasped.

"Yeah, he sure did."

She bent over, hands flat against her thighs. "I need to talk to you."

"What about?"

She rolled her eyes, her body heaving for breath. "You know what about."

"Why don't you tell me." I crossed my arms. "Or, I know, I can get a psychic to read your mind."

"Stop." She gulped air. Finally she straightened up. "Can I come inside?"

I rocked back and forth for a minute. Then I walked back to the house and let her in.

She sank onto the couch. I stood in front of the windowed wall and crossed my arms again. My heartbeat drummed in my head.

"What did Kent tell you?" she asked.

"Why? You need to get your story straight?"

She sighed and leaned forward, pulling at the wisps of hair that hung over her forehead. "I just want to know how much I need to explain."

"How about *all of it*?"

She closed her eyes. "You probably think I'm a big liar. But I didn't mean to lie to you."

"That's a good one," I said. "What did you mean to do?"

"I don't know. I just—I wanted things to *fit*."

"What the hell are you talking about?"

"I mean, I know what really happened, but it seems wrong to me." Her eyes opened. "It doesn't make sense. Like . . ."

"Like what?" I snapped when she didn't go on.

"Well, like—why didn't my dad write a note that meant something?"

"Oh, yeah. The note," I said. The thought of that note scratched up another spark inside me. "The note you said didn't exist."

"All right, there was a note, but not a real note."

"What do you mean, 'real'?"

"All it said was 'sorry' and 'I can't take this anymore.' It didn't tell me what I needed to know. It didn't say *anything*." She swallowed. "So I had a note, but it felt like I didn't have a note."

She waited, but when I didn't say anything, she went on. "And—the waterfall. Why would he pick such a beautiful place?"

"Why the hell not?" I had picked a garage because it was the only enclosed space I knew of where the car would fit. I would rather have picked someplace like the waterfall. If I had to pick a place.

"Why would he take Matt and Kent with him, but not me? And why did he take me to Funworld and not them?" Her face, which had started to pale to its normal color, flushed again. "Was he playing favorites?"

Her question hung in the air. In my mind I added the next question, which she didn't ask: *And if so, who were the favorites— Nicki or the boys? The kid he took to Funworld or the kids he took with him on his last trip to the waterfall?*

She said, "None of it makes sense. The pieces don't fit. And that's why it didn't feel like lying when I told you—"

"It felt like lying to me."

She looked up at me then, her eyes huge. "I'm sorry, Ryan."

I didn't answer for a minute. So much had knotted up inside me that I couldn't pull out any single thread and identify it.

Then I said, "I trusted you. I don't trust anyone, but I trusted you."

"I—"

"I must've been out of my mind. It's my own fucking fault— there's a reason I never believe in anyone or—"

"*I just wanted it to make sense!*"

That cut off the breath in my throat. Her words lay in the middle of the room.

I knew what she meant. I wasn't ready to admit it yet, but I knew.

"You want a glass of water?" My voice came out rough, and my hands shook, but I was cooling a little.

"Yeah. Please."

She watched me cross the room, enter the kitchen, and stand over the sink. I poured her a glass of water and dropped in two ice cubes. She winced when they cracked.

I came back and handed her the drink.

"I couldn't tell you about the waterfall," she said. "I thought maybe you would get creeped out and wouldn't meet me there anymore." She sipped her water, still watching me. "And I have to go to the waterfall. Nobody understands that—not even Kent, who goes there all the time, too. He says it's just to get high, but come on, he could get high plenty of other places."

I watched the ice cubes bump against each other in her drink. "How come you picked me to talk to, anyway? Was it—'he's just the psycho kid, so who cares what I tell him?'"

"No! I picked you because—because I thought you would understand." Her eyes were gray, flecked with black. They didn't look away from me. "Not only because you tried the same thing he did, but because you were always at the waterfall. It's like I was meant to meet you."

"Hey, according to your friends, you're just 'being nice to the local loser.'"

"What friends? What are you talking about?"

"That skinny girl with the long hair who lives down on Maybrook, the guy who hangs around with her and wears that skeleton T-shirt—"

"Amanda and J.T.? They're not my friends. We used to eat lunch together in eighth grade and they think they still know me, but they don't."

Moisture dripped off the glass she held, welled up between her fingers. I focused on that, to keep from looking at her eyes again.

"It's the truth," she said. "Do you think I would tell them about my dad? About Funworld? Do you think they know *any* of the stuff I've told you?"

I wanted to believe her, but I couldn't. My gut told me to trust her, but my brain, which was still unraveling her lies, thought that was crazy. I attacked on another front. "Why the fuck did we drive all over the state to talk to those psychics?"

She took another drink and set the glass on the carpet. "You know why."

"No, I really don't."

"I wanted to find my father. Like I told you." She wiped her hand on her shorts. "Not that they had any answers. So I kept coming back to you." Again the pleading look.

I breathed in hard, hating that expression on her face, the belief she always had that I could speak for her father. That *responsibility*. More than anything, I could not handle that responsibility.

"Bullshit," I said.

"Seriously. Whatever I've learned about my dad—at least, why he did what he did—I learned it from you."

I turned to the windows and faced the trees outside, the ferns, the sunlight filtered through green branches. The more I was tempted to forgive Nicki, the more it hurt. As if I were being pulled apart by inches, each cell stretched to its tearing point. Every alarm bell in my body clanged, warning me not to let her in again. With what she knew about me, she could rip my skin off in front of the neighborhood, spread my guts on the ground for them all to sneer at.

"I don't want to be your—suicide guru," I said. "I'm sick of you."

"I don't mean—"

"Is that why you made out with me? Is that why you told me about Funworld? Just trying to squeeze more information out of me?" I turned back to her. "Well, fuck that. You got everything already."

She stood and took a step toward me, her foot knocking over the glass. Water spread across the carpet, but neither of us bothered with it. Instead she straightened her back and said, "I did *not* trick you. You know I didn't. Maybe I was scared to tell you some of the real details, but all the important stuff was true. My father *is* dead, and he *did* kill himself, and I *don't* know why. And everything I told you about Funworld was true." She swallowed. "And I kissed you because I wanted to kiss you. Because I like you. Sometimes I think I could like you a lot, if you'd let me. And I can't understand why that stupid Val didn't have the brains to kiss you herself."

We were both breathing hard now, as if we'd been running on the trail or had just come up from under the pounding of the waterfall. I wanted to believe her and at the same time I didn't want to trust her, didn't want to risk it.

And so I didn't let up.

"Why did you make up the part about the gun? About you and Matt finding him?"

"Matt was there with Dad. But I told you it was me instead of

Kent because I wished I was there." Her face went blank for a second, then flushed, and she sobbed. Her sob made me shudder. "Some people think that's sick, but I don't mean I wanted to see him die. I wanted to be there, I wanted to be there for him—you know, like people go to the hospital and say good-bye when people die there?"

She gasped, wiping her face on the back of her hand. "Nobody thinks that's strange," she said. "Everyone hangs over the hospital bed, and nobody thinks that's strange."

I wanted to touch her, stop her crying, stroke her hair, but I didn't. Or couldn't. My right hand trembled, but that was as much as I could move.

She sniffled, licked tears from her lips. And then she bent down to pick up the ice on the carpet.

"I'm sorry," she said, ice cubes clinking into the glass. "I'm sorry."

I inched over until I was right in front of her, the soggy rug squishing under my feet.

"Nicki," I said. I reached out, slowly. But she jumped up, grabbed my hand, and pulled me closer to her.

I wrapped my arms around her. She pressed her face against my shirt, and her tears wet my shoulder. The air-conditioning hummed in the background, a white noise I usually didn't even notice.

Her sobs quieted to sniffles. "I guess you think I'm crazy," she said.

"I'm not one to judge."

We both laughed a little. She sighed and let me go.

"Who's Bruce Macauley?" I asked.

"What?"

"That's who you said died at the waterfall. Did you make up that name?"

She stared past me for a minute, then laughed. "I forgot I used that name. He was a kid I knew in second grade. He moved away that year—thank God. He used to kill frogs and squirrels, and he was always throwing rocks at my friends and me."

I brought towels from the kitchen, and we spread them over the spill on the living-room floor.

Nicki followed me out onto the porch. The day had turned hot, the sun heavy on our faces and shoulders. I leaned against the porch railing, facing the trees. I felt her watching me and glanced over. "What?" I said.

She shook her head, as if to say, *Nothing.* But she kept looking, studying me.

It was like being seen for the first time. Whenever I was behind the glass wall, I felt invisible, even though glass is supposed to be transparent. I'd been invisible back in the library; nobody had noticed me stealing a sweater in broad fluorescent light. I'd been invisible at my new school, except for whatever attention the suicide rumors brought me. Having people know *about* you wasn't the same thing as having them *know* you, though.

But Nicki saw me.

"I'm never going to know what happened with my dad, am I?" she said, standing near me. She had a scent like wood and citrus and pine needles. I didn't think she used perfume.

"Probably not."

"Let me ask you something." She rubbed the head of a nail on the porch railing.

"What?"

"Do you ever—still think about killing yourself?"

"No," I said automatically, because that's what I always said when Dr. Briggs asked me. It's what I told my parents whenever they asked.

Then I said, "Sometimes." I paused. "Yeah, I do."

After all, who was I kidding? I'd been thinking about it less than an hour ago.

"Why?" she asked.

"I don't know. When things get rough, it kind of flashes through my mind. I haven't been serious about it for a long time, and I'm nowhere near doing it, but I think about it."

I had never admitted that to anyone. I was scared that if I told my parents or Dr. Briggs, they would lock me up again. My parents, for sure, would never trust me. They barely trusted me as it was. But it was always an option—an option I'd moved very far down the list, but which sat in my back pocket like the emergency bus token I used to carry around West Seaton. Just in case.

Nicki touched my back, at first so lightly I could barely feel it. When I didn't move, she let her hand rest there more solidly. I closed my eyes, savoring the sun on my skin. And Nicki's touch, the way the two of us were separated only by the thin cotton of my shirt.

■ ■ ■ ■ ■

My father came home that night, and he fell asleep while we watched another baseball game. He didn't even wake up in the eighth inning, when I called for a walk on a star batter. The batter hit a home run.

"Told you to walk him," I said to the TV, fishing the last of our popcorn out from among the hard unpopped nuggets. Dad snored on.

He woke up at the top of the ninth, during a pitching change. "Who's winning?"

"Tie score."

"Oh." He rubbed his face, which was gray with stubble, then took off his glasses and rubbed his eyes. "Looks like I woke up just in time."

One of the beer commercials showed a guy jumping out of a plane. "I'm going to do that for my eighteenth birthday," I said.

Dad put his glasses back on. He had gotten a special kind of glass that didn't reflect, so I could see his eyes as if the frames were empty, as if the lenses didn't exist. "You're still thinking about that?"

"Yeah. I looked it up again—you have to be eighteen. So I'll do it then."

"You'll give your mother a heart attack."

"That won't be *all* my fault."

I didn't think before I said that. The words seemed to smack my dad's face in slow motion. They surprised me, too.

"What do you mean?" he said.

"You don't think she has problems?" I'd been thinking of myself as the sick one for so long that it was only now I let myself acknowledge how close to the edge my mother lived, tightly controlling everything, for fear of—what? I thought of her treadmilling in the middle of the night, chopping her food symmetrically. It wasn't just about me and that night in the garage. She'd been this way ever since I could remember. "She's kind of . . . tightly wound." I couldn't believe I had to explain. He must've noticed.

He frowned. "Your mother is a worrier. She's always been an anxious person." And I hadn't helped—I'd given her something to worry about, all right. "But she's always been there for you. You're the main reason she took a job where she could work from home."

"I thought it was so she could have quality time with this house."

"Don't be ridiculous. She did it for you." His voice had a weird edge, rough like a serrated knife. "She thought—after Patterson— that I should travel less, spend more time here." He paused, then said the next words so carefully I could almost hear him picking them, shaping them in his mind. "But she decided to work at home, and I thought it wouldn't be good for us to smother you. I thought it would be better if my schedule went back to normal."

"You were right." Not that I would've minded seeing my father more. But if they'd both spent the summer hovering over me, watching every breath I took, I probably would've been back in the hospital long before Jake.

On the other hand, if Dad stayed home more, would Mom relax more? How come *she* had to be my full-time babysitter? Wouldn't she like the chance to get away from here sometimes, to fly across the ocean herself?

But I couldn't imagine her relaxed, without the tension that made the air practically twang whenever she was in the room. I told Dad, "All I'm saying is, maybe she should spend less time worrying about me, and more time worrying about herself."

The game had come back on, the announcers deep into their soothing drone. The count was two and two.

"Ryan, your mother has always been high-strung. But she never stockpiled enough drugs to kill herself. She never started a car in a closed garage." He pushed his glasses higher on his nose. "And she's not the only one who's concerned about this skydiving idea. I think you should talk to Dr. Briggs about it. About—why you want to do it."

"Fine." From the TV came a crack and a roar: base hit. "I know why I want to do it, though."

"Why?" He sounded hoarse, strangled, like he had a popcorn kernel stuck in his throat.

"Because it would be like flying." I turned back to the TV. Just before I punched up the volume on the remote, I added, "I'm gonna pull the cord, you know."

"What?" he said.

"Nothing." But I was pretty sure he'd heard me.

TWENTY-TWO

On Saturday Mom drove me back to Patterson. In the car, I said, "I know about Jake cutting his wrists."

"Oh," she said.

"You could've told me."

Her knuckles paled on the steering wheel. I watched them while I waited for her answer.

"That's not an easy thing for me to talk about, Ryan," she said. "It hits a little too close to home."

After a minute, I said, "I know, but I don't see the point of pretending it didn't happen."

"I'm not pretending. I would just rather we focused on more positive things. I don't think it's healthy to dwell on . . ."

I waited for the end of that sentence, but all she did was sigh. Then she said, "I want you to have a good environment, good influences. If we can control that—"

"But you can't control it."

Again, her knuckles went yellow with strain.

"You can't control everything I hear and everyone I meet and everything that happens to me."

For a long time, I wasn't sure that she'd heard me. But finally she laughed and said, under her breath, "That's exactly what I hate."

I sat with Jake in the dayroom, which had been painted a depressing dark mustard color. They'd given me a visitor's badge at the front desk, and I kept having the strange feeling that I should take it off, that my old counselors would see me and ask who I was trying to fool. And yet I knew I didn't belong there anymore.

Jake's arms were heavy with bandages. He picked at the tape, and I thought of the cuts underneath, the rough edges of skin sewn together, the hot red scabs that probably made his arms ache even now. I was glad he was alive, that his body had refused to bleed out.

And I was glad it wasn't me. Glad my arms were smooth and whole, that I could get up and walk out of this hospital anytime I wanted.

"This new med makes my tongue weigh ten pounds," he slurred. "Is it swelling up?" He stuck out his tongue.

"Nah, it looks normal."

He worked his mouth, swallowed. I remembered the dry mouth I'd gotten from my prescription when I first went on it. "You want something to drink?" I asked.

Val rushed in. "Oh my God, look at these walls. This is the ugliest color I've ever seen." She kissed Jake's cheek. "How are you?"

"Shitty."

"Ryan's mother and mine are downstairs. Is it okay if they come up and say hello? They want to see you."

He hesitated.

"You don't have to," I said.

"Good," he said. "'Cause—I don't really want to."

Val sat on his other side. There we were, the three of us in a row, just like the old days. Except everything was different now, and we all knew it.

"Guess I flunk," Jake said.

"What?" Val asked.

"We all graduated from this place, right? Except I'm the only one who had to come back."

"It's not flunking," she told him. "Don't you dare think about it that way."

He turned his face away from her. "I wish I had a cheeseburger."

"I'll get you one." I stood up, relieved at the chance to get away from Val.

Jake gave me half a smile. "With everything on it. Give me something to live for, man."

"It's only a cheeseburger," I said, "but I'll do what I can."

I went down the block and got it, along with fries, and a large soda for his dry mouth. I fought off the mothers' questions in the lobby. My mother didn't kill me on sight, so I guessed that Dr. Ishihara hadn't mentioned my visit to Val yet. I could imagine what Mom would do if she heard that Nicki had driven me to Brookfield.

When I came back into the dayroom, Jake was bent over Val's lap, hanging on her, while she stroked his hair. I hung back, watching, and the way he clawed at her made me wonder if maybe I hadn't been the only one in love with Val all this time.

Val noticed me first; then Jake lifted his head. "Hey, it's my reason to live," he said when he saw the bag in my hand.

I crossed the room. "Well, it does smell pretty good."

He straightened up, wiped a hand across his face, and took the bag. Val patted his shoulder and said, "I'll be right back."

As soon as she'd gone, he bit into a fry. "It wasn't what it looked like," he said.

"What do you mean?"

"She doesn't like me that way. She always liked you."

"Not enough," I said. "She made that pretty clear last week." It stung to admit that, but at least it no longer felt like my guts were being scraped out an inch at a time.

He sighed and kept eating. Val came back and sat with us, the three of us quiet, the way we'd learned to be with each other months earlier. It was funny—I wouldn't want to live at Patterson again, but for a few minutes I missed what we'd had when we all lived there, when we saw each other every day.

Jake finished his burger, slurping up the last bit of onion and tomato. Then he said, "I don't know how to do this. I don't know why you and Val figured it out and I can't."

"I haven't figured out anything," I said. "I'm just making it up as I go along."

"Me, too," Val said.

Jake held out the rest of the fries to us. "I always feel like there's some rule book everyone else got that I never got."

Val and I laughed. We hadn't gotten the book, either.

"I'm sick of feeling like crap," he said.

Val touched his knee. "It gets better."

"Oh, yeah? When?"

"I don't know. But it does."

He crumpled up the empty bag. "For everyone but me."

I remembered feeling that way, that night in the garage. And again on the way home from Val's after she'd rejected me. And every time I'd had to look at that stupid pink sweater in my closet. And when I'd found out that Nicki had lied to me. Every time I thought things might be okay, the ground caved in under my feet.

But then, like Val said, things got better. And worse again. And better. I was beginning to see this wave of ups and downs stretching out in front of me forever, beginning to think maybe that was just life.

"If you hang on," Val said, "I promise you it does get better."

Jake's hand shook. He crushed the balled-up bag tighter. "Bull," he said, but his voice shook, too, and I knew he wanted to believe her.

He turned to me. "Does it get better?"

That was the question, and I owed him Patterson Honesty. And so I gave it to him.

"Yes," I said.

Late that afternoon, I returned to the waterfall. I didn't go under the cascade. I dunked myself in the pool and watched water pour over rock. I put everything I knew about Nicki and her father back together, tried to replace the lies with the truth. It wasn't always easy to remember which puzzle pieces belonged, or to put the new pieces in place of the old.

When Nicki showed up on the bank with four other kids who lived along the highway, I almost ducked under the water, but I knew I couldn't hold my breath until they left. I recognized a couple of them from the bus stop last year—not that I'd spoken to them. I used to sit alone on a rock, with earbuds on. Some of the time, I didn't even have any music on. I wore the earbuds because they gave me an excuse not to talk to anyone, and they gave everyone else an obvious reason not to have to talk to me.

Now the kids settled on a clump of fallen trees well back from the water's edge, talking, smoking. The girl who'd called me the "local loser" wasn't there. Nicki looked from me to her friends, as if not sure where she belonged.

I splashed out of the water and toweled off, dripping on the moss, feeling their eyes on me. If I walked away without speaking, they wouldn't think it was unusual. They probably didn't expect anything else from me at this point.

And what about Nicki?

She had said, *I think I could like you a lot, if you'd let me,* and I had been running those words through my mind, over and over, rubbing them smooth like beach stones. I could've said those same words about Val. But every time I saw or talked to Val now, I felt the space between us widening.

I think I could like you a lot.

I met Nicki's eyes, and she glanced away instantly, the way drops of water ricochet off a hot pan.

I thought I could like her a lot. Maybe I already did.

In spite of everything. Maybe because of everything. Because we both knew what it was like to feel bad and choose the wrong way to cope with it. Because we'd both covered up things we couldn't stand to admit. Because we both wanted to believe there was such a thing as forgiveness.

I crumpled my towel and walked over to the group. I said hi and they nodded back, made a few jokes about school starting next week, offered me a smoke. I'd forgotten what it was like to talk to people—casually, at least—to bullshit about ordinary stuff. But after a few minutes the rust flaked off my voice, and I managed to sound something like a human being.

Nicki sat silent, her face flushing every time I looked at her. A wisp of hair blew across her cheek, and I wanted to brush it away.

"Want to take a walk?" I asked her. I hadn't thought her face could get redder, but it did then.

"Yes."

We said good-bye to the others and took the path that led to my house. As soon as we were alone, she said, "I'm really sorry I lied to you."

I nodded. "I'm sorry you lost your dad." After a pause: "You know that what he did wasn't your fault, right?"

"Most of the time I know it."

"Well, it's true. It was him, not you."

"Thanks," she said, so softly I almost missed it.

I rubbed my tongue against the roof of my mouth, looking for any moisture, anything to help get the next words out.

"What?" she said, and I shook my head. She stopped then, so I stopped, too, and we faced each other. Mostly what I wanted to do was touch her, her arm or maybe her back, the way she'd touched me on the deck.

I didn't know exactly what we were to each other, but I didn't have to stick a label on it yet, either. I needed Val's shadow to fade more before I could be sure, but I thought I knew what I would find when it did fade. I willed my hand to move, and for a second it seemed like the pane of glass was back, blocking me, but my hand twitched. And even though my arm was stiff and heavy, I managed to lift it and rest my hand on Nicki's shoulder. I ran my thumb along the seam in her shirt. She touched the back of my neck, rubbed the cool skin where water seeped down from my hair. "You're shivering," she said.

"I know."

My hand shook, but I wasn't numb. I felt the roughness of the fabric and the warmth of her body, the slight rise her shoulder made with every breath. I realized I wasn't the only one shivering. We leaned into each other, and I bent to rest my forehead against hers. Scared as I was to be that close to her, I stayed there, my skin touching hers. I didn't move away.

ACKNOWLEDGMENTS

Many thanks to everyone at the Curtis Brown agency, especially Ginger Knowlton and Anna Umansky; and to the crew at Viking and Penguin, especially Leila Sales. I am grateful for the guidance provided by Catherine Frank and Nathan Bransford. I appreciate not only the outstanding professional skills of everyone mentioned here, but also the fact that they are a joy to work with.

A big *thank-you* to the critiquers who helped me improve this book: Tracy Dickens, Jessica Dimuzio (VMD), Carmen Ferreiro-Esteban, Laurel Garver, Colleen Rowan Kosinski, and Molly Lorenz. I greatly appreciate the support and friendship of fellow writers Lisa Brackmann, Angela De Groot, Kelly Fineman, and Julia Hoban. A group hug goes to the communities who have helped me so much: Debut2009, the Tenners, the 2k classes, the Milestones Critique Circle of Chestnut Hill, and the Kidlit Authors Club. Thanks to gracious writing-retreat hosts James and Martha Bosco. I acknowledge with gratitude that R.E.M. inspired this book's title.

Loving thanks to my family and friends, especially my parents, Jim and Cheryl; my sister, Bonnie; my grandmothers, Dorothy and Jane; and my stepson, Will. Most of all, to my husband, John: deepest love and thanks for always being there, and for always being wonderful.

Finally, for those who need to hear this: things *can* get better. They can even start getting better today.

Turn the page for a preview
of Jennifer R. Hubbard's

the secret year

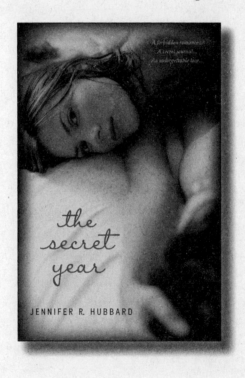

◼ *chapter 1* ◼

Julia was killed on Labor Day on her way home from a party. I didn't get to see her that night. I used to meet her on Friday nights, but I was never invited to the parties that she was invited to. We'd meet on the banks of the river, clutch at each other in the backseat of her car, steam up her windows and write messages and jokes to each other in the fog on the glass, and argue about whether to turn on the A/C. Sometimes we swam in the river late at night when the water was black and no one could see us. We did all that for a year, and nobody else knew.

There were a couple of reasons we never told anybody about us. For one thing, she lived up on Black Mountain Road, in a house that was five times as big as mine. With servants. And a computerized alarm system that looked like it should've been running the space program instead of protecting one house. At my place, we just had a sign my father tacked up in our yard that said TRESPASSERS WILL BE SHOT.

We didn't have anything worth stealing anyway. I lived on the flats off Higgins Farm Road, where there were no farms left anymore, in a house with my father's junked cars all over the yard. Every couple of years the township gave my dad a ticket and tried to get him to clear out our property, but he basically told them to go to hell. When I was little, I liked to play in those cars. I used to imagine I could help get them running again. But by the time I was fifteen, I realized those wrecks were never going to move again unless they were dragging behind a tow truck.

Anyway, that was the biggest difference between Julia and me: Black Mountain versus the flats. Not that we were Romeo and Juliet or anything. Nobody was trying to keep us apart. My family wouldn't have cared if I'd gone out with her. Julia's family probably would've hated me, but they wouldn't have locked her in her room. It was what her friends would've thought that bothered her, I think. Besides, she already had a boyfriend: Austin Chadwick. His name always sounded fake to me, like the kind an actor would give himself. She was with him that last night.

Austin lived on Black Mountain, too, with his expensive car and his expensive clothes. I have to admit, though, the cars and clothes didn't bother me as much as the way he strutted around like he was *entitled* to what he had, instead of realizing he was born into it, dumb-ass lucky.

Was I jealous that he could go anywhere he wanted with Julia, that they ate at the same lunch table and made out in front of the drinking fountain? Hell, no. I didn't want to be her boyfriend. Things were better the way they were. She used to drive down to the bridge near my house in her little black car, and I'd meet her there. I guess I would've liked to *talk* to her at school, though. Not to have to pretend we didn't know each other. When she passed me in the halls, her eyes would glide over me like I was part of the walls. That turned me cold. I liked to break that glide, to catch and hold her eyes.

Usually nobody else was looking, but once her friend Pam noticed. She nudged Julia, leaned in, and whispered in her ear. Julia laughed and flipped her hair back as if to say, "Who, that guy? I was just staring into space, and he happened to be in the way."

I heard about the accident a few hours after it happened. It was Labor Day—night, actually. The house was too quiet because my brother, Tom, had just gone off to his first year of college. I wasn't used to the stillness yet. Before, I had always heard his stereo, or his hammering away at weird projects, like the twelve-foot abstract wooden "sculpture" he built in the backyard.

I was on my bed, listening to the rain and trying to decide whether to go into the kitchen for another bowl of cornflakes (and hear my mother say for the ten millionth time, "Colten, do you have a tapeworm?") or keep lying there and fall asleep, which would mean waking up starving around two in the morning.

The phone rang then. I rolled over to grab it. "Colt?" my friend Sydney said. I knew she recognized my voice, but she always sounded tentative, as if she might've dialed the wrong number.

"Hi, Syd."

"Did you hear about the accident?"

"What accident?"

"Up on Black Mountain Road. Julia Vernon got killed, and Pam Henderson's in the hospital."

I sat up. "Who told you that?"

"Kirby. The Hendersons called her to babysit Pam's brother when they went to the hospital."

I got out of bed and started to walk up and down the space between my bed and desk. "Are you sure?"

"All I know is what Kirby said. She seemed pretty sure."

I didn't say anything. I kept pacing.

"I bet they were drunk. There was a big party at Adam Hancock's all day—his parents are in Greece."

"Were they in Austin's car? Was he with them?"

"No, it was just the two of them, in Pam's car."

Well, they sure as hell couldn't have been in Julia's. I knew her car was in the shop, and I also knew why, but I couldn't tell Syd any of that.

"What else did you hear?" I asked.

"Not much. But Kirby thinks Pam is going to be okay."

Syd wasn't part of the Black Mountain crowd any more than I was. After all, she lived on the flats, and she hung around with people like me. But she kept tabs on the Black Mountain kids as if she were a reporter for a celebrity gossip show. Syd got her information from friends like Kirby Matthews, who lived at the base of Black Mountain and didn't fully belong to either the mountain or the flats crowd. Most of the time, when Syd told me the latest from the grapevine, I couldn't care less. That night I did care. That night I wanted to know everything.

I got off the phone with Syd as soon as I realized she didn't know any more than she'd said already. I called Julia's cell phone. I had never done that unless I was sure she wanted me to and sure she'd be alone. Now I called anyway. I wanted her to tell me the gossip was wrong, that she was fine. I would've even been happy to have her pissed at me for calling.

Nobody answered. I got her usual message. "Hi there, it's Julia, and my phone's off because I'm the only person in the world who doesn't want the rest of civilization listening to my calls. Leave a message, the juicier the better, extra points for creativity, and I'll listen to it when I'm alone." I hung up before the beep and sat on my bed, trying to figure out what to do next.

I couldn't help thinking of the last time we'd seen each other, the fight we'd had. We'd made up afterward, but it was one of those fights where the other person's words burn right into you, where apologies don't keep them from scarring. But I didn't want to think about that now. So even though all the details threatened to rise up and run through my head again, I squashed them down. I focused on trying to find out what had happened, whether she was really dead.

I had an old black-and-white TV in my room. "Museum quality," my brother Tom always joked, but it was good enough to get me the eleven o'clock news. Yes, there had been an accident on Black Mountain Road. They showed the car, gnarled metal that looked like it could've once been Pam Henderson's car. One fatality, the passenger. The driver had been taken to the hospital. No names were being released yet.

One fatality, the passenger. I knew then. But some part of me didn't believe it, and in the days after that I kept waiting for more information, waiting for the story to change. Even when everybody knew she was dead, when the obituary came out and the funeral was scheduled, I kept expecting to see her in town, at school, at the bridge. Late at night, I'd call her cell number just to hear her voice in that recorded message. It took a few weeks for her parents to cut off the service. Every time I called, I was scared somebody in her family would answer the phone, but they never did.

Rumors about the accident filled the school halls. People said Julia was drunk that night but Pam wasn't. Pam came out of the accident with a broken arm and a concussion. She supposedly told her friends that Julia wasn't strapped in because she kept leaning out the window to throw up. I wasn't a friend of Pam's, so I never heard anything firsthand.

They said Pam went so crazy over the whole thing, seeing Julia die and all, that they shipped her off to a different school this year. I didn't know how much of that was true, about Pam going crazy, but she wasn't at the funeral. I managed to go; you didn't need an invitation for that. Nobody asked me what I was doing there because so many kids from school had come, even people who hardly knew Julia. I stayed in the back.

Austin was there. Julia told me she was going to break up with him at the party, but she'd said that before. If she did break up with him, he sure didn't show it. He stood with her family, held her mother's hand, patted her brother's shoulder. He went up to put a rose on her casket right after her mother did. He even stroked the surface of the casket like it was Julia's skin.

I knew Julia, but nobody else knew that. We were good at keeping secrets. So after Labor Day weekend, I was the only one who knew about us.

chapter 2

At school I always hung out with the same guys, all of us from the flats. Nick drove us in his car, now that we were juniors and could park in the good spaces in the north parking lot. We had to wait until the third week for him to take us, though, because his mother caught him drinking at the end of the summer and took away his keys for a while.

Nick and Paul sat up front, as usual. I was squished in the back with Syd and Fred. My legs took up so much room that Syd had to sit on my lap. As Nick zoomed around the curve that led into the center of town, showing off, I said, "How about giving us a chance to reach our senior year?"

"You can drive from all the way back there, huh, Morrissey?" he said. "Pretty damn good for someone without a license."

"Ten points for that squirrel," Paul said.

"You didn't really hit a squirrel, did you?" Syd asked.

"No." Nick laughed.

Blood rushed through my body, surging from one side to the other as Nick whipped us around corners. I swallowed to keep my stomach where it belonged. The heat of our bodies crammed together didn't help. We reached school just in time, as far as I was concerned. Another mile and I would've been showing everybody what I had for breakfast.

Usually I wasn't the carsick type. But I couldn't stop thinking about Julia's head exploding as it slammed into the windshield of Pam's car. Thinking and trying not to think, wondering if she felt it or if she was too drunk to know what hit her.

Julia's brother, Michael, was a sophomore. I hadn't said twenty words to him in my life, so I wasn't expecting him to speak up behind me in the cafeteria line. I hadn't seen him back there. "You're Colten Morrissey, right?" he said.

I swung my head around when he spoke. My skin prickled. If I hadn't already known who he was, I might have guessed. The ghost of Julia looked out of his eyes, was there in the bones of his face. He was skinnier than she had been, though—scrawny, even. He wore glasses, and his chin jutted out more. And while her hair had been a reddish brown, his was much darker.

"Yeah," I said. "Why?"

"I was wondering." He took something wrapped in a tortilla that our cafeteria called a "quesadilla," and put it on his tray. "You had a few classes with my sister, didn't you?"

"Uh, yeah, when I was a freshman." What had made him connect me with Julia?

He plunked a bowl of vanilla pudding onto his tray. I took a plate of something without looking at it and slid my tray along the rails.

"Which classes? Math, I believe? With Bruckner?"

"Calvert."

He snapped his fingers. "Calvert. That's right." We stopped at the drink station. He took a glass and held it under the juice spout. I watched red liquid trickle out for a minute and then forced myself to get a glass of water.

"Was Carlos Mendez in that class, too?" he said.

"Mendez? No."

"Oh."

Why the hell was he asking all this? I waited for him to explain, but he just watched his juice pour as if he'd never seen anything so fascinating. "It's almost empty," he muttered, as the flow slowed to a dribble.

"Michael—"

He looked up at me. "You came to the funeral, didn't you?"

"Yes."

"That was nice of you. Considering you didn't know her very well." I just stood there, and he moved around me to the cashier. I followed him then, an electric hum in my brain, a queasy heat rising up from my stomach. I didn't know exactly what he was after, but I didn't like it. After he'd paid for his own lunch, he waited for me to finish with the cashier. I saw him waiting and wished he'd get lost—sink through the floor, fly out the window, anything. But he was still there when I got through the line.

"You can stop squirming," he said. "I'm not going to tell anyone."

Shit. I kept my face blank. "Not going to tell anyone what?"

He gave me a thin smile and shook his head. "Are you going to play stupid now? When I mentioned my sister, you panicked."

"I don't—"

"Maybe nobody else would notice, but I can read faces." He sipped his juice. "Besides, you've just confirmed a few other things for me." He glanced around, but there was no one near us. "I know about the letters. I know you're C.M."

This time I could honestly say, "Michael, I don't know what the hell you're talking about."

"Well, I don't believe that, but never mind." He stared at me as if he could peel off my skin with his eyes. "I have something for you from my sister. If you're interested, meet me outside the east entrance after school." He took his tray to a table in the corner without giving me another look.

I went to my usual table, numb. *I know about the letters.* What letters? He obviously knew something about Julia and me, or thought he did, but whatever code he was speaking, I didn't get it. I had no idea what he wanted to give me, either. A picture of Julia? A lock of her hair? A punch in the face?

I made sure not to look over at the table of Black Mountain royalty, where Austin Chadwick sat, where Julia used to sit. I had gotten so used to avoiding her at school that now I avoided even the spaces she should have filled. But today I had another reason; I didn't want them to see whatever Michael Vernon had supposedly seen on my face.

I checked out the rest of my table to see if anyone else thought I was easy to read. Syd picked through her salad as if checking for bugs. Fred was trying to do his homework for his afternoon classes. Paul wasn't there—probably making out with his girlfriend behind the school. Nick leaned over and gawked at the sandwich on my tray.

"What is that, turkey?"

"I guess."

"You shoulda got the roast beef." He lifted his own sandwich, mayo oozing out onto his fingers.

"Something wrong, Colt?" Syd asked.

"Like what?"

She shrugged. "I don't know. You look a little off. Like you're having second thoughts about the turkey."

I shoved Michael and Julia to the back of my mind. "I'm not sure it *is* turkey." I poked the sandwich. "It's more of a turkeylike substance."

"Good point," she said, and went back to her salad.

I took a breath. "I can't ride home with you guys today," I told Nick.

"What, you got detention?"

"Yeah."

"Well," he said, grinning around a mouthful of roast beef, "enjoy the bus." And none of them gave any sign that they knew I was lying.

I didn't hear anything that went on in my afternoon classes. The teachers could've scheduled three tests for the next day, and I wouldn't have known it. All I did was watch the clock hands creep around to the final bell.

Michael was waiting for me, right where he'd said. He smiled grimly. "So, you've decided you did know Julia after all."

I didn't answer.

He pulled something out of his backpack and held it up: a purple notebook with a diagonal black stripe across its cover.

"What's that?" I asked.

"Come on. I know you're C.M."

"I'm what?"

"*C.M.* The C.M. she wrote all these letters to."

Letters? I couldn't stop staring at that book. Julia used to write me short notes sometimes ("Meet me at the bridge tonight"), always unsigned, slipped through the vent in my locker. But I didn't know anything about any letters.

"I put the clues together," he said. "It wasn't difficult. She mentioned that you lived on the flats, near Higgins Farm Bridge. She also wrote that you were younger than she was, and that you'd been in Calvert's class with her." He paused to adjust his glasses. "The only other person it could have been was Carlos Mendez, and I've ruled him out."

I wanted to know what was in that notebook, but he was only holding it up, not handing it over. For a second, I wondered if he might not even show it to me, just hold it over my head. Not that he had a reputation for that kind of viciousness, but he was definitely strange.

Nobody could figure Michael out or predict what he might do. Julia had told me a few things about him: He'd painted the ceiling of his room black. He'd taken pictures of potatoes for his freshman art project. He'd once fasted for a week as part of a report on Gandhi. I also remembered that he'd tried to start an ethics and philosophy club at school last year, but he couldn't get anyone to join. None of those facts helped me guess what he was up to now.

"You've really never seen this book before?" he asked.

"No."

"But you knew my sister." It wasn't a question. His eyes nailed me to the wall, reminding me of an old insect collection my science teacher had once shown us, bugs splayed out and frozen with pins.

"Yes," I said. It was the first time I'd admitted it to anyone.

He handed me the notebook. "Then you might as well look."

I opened it to the first page. It was Julia's, all right: black ink on lavender pages, each word bold and dark, the same writing I used to find on notes in my locker.

> Dear C.M.,
>   I had to write this down because I don't believe what just happened.

I recognized the date: the first night I'd ever met her at the bridge, last September.

I closed the book because I didn't want to read more in front of him. "Why are you showing this to me?"

"I thought about throwing it away," he said. "Burning it, pretending it never existed. But I know what Julia would've wanted. She—" He cut himself off, and swallowed. "Well. Read it if you want. I believe that's why she wrote it." He turned and walked away. He was halfway across the school lawn before I realized I probably should've thanked him.